AF472279

SECOND CHANCE

BY: ROBERT V. WARD, JR.

PUBLISHED FEBRUARY, 2012

AVAILABLE AT LULU.COM

SECOND CHANCE

Dedication

Charles Hamilton Houston, attorney and Dean of Howard University School of Law was fond of saying, “Lawyers can either be parasites or social engineers.”

This story is dedicated to the “social engineers” who labored tirelessly to protect the social and economic rights of all. It is they who work daily to secure dignity and justice for everyone. Without them, there would be no second chances.

42 USC § 1983

1983. Civil Action For Deprivation of Rights

Every person who, under color of any statute, ordinance, regulation, custom, or usage, of any State or Territory or the District of Columbia, subjects, or causes to be subjected, any citizen of the United States or other person within the jurisdiction thereof to the deprivation of any rights, privileges, or immunities secured by the Constitution and laws, shall be liable to the party injured in an action at law, suit in equity, or other proper proceeding for redress, except that in any action brought against a judicial officer for an act or omission taken in such officer's judicial capacity, injunctive relief shall not be granted unless a declaratory decree was violated or declaratory relief was unavailable. For the purposes of this section, any Act of Congress applicable exclusively to the District of Columbia shall be considered to be a statute of the District of Columbia.

SECOND CHANCE

Prologue

It was a balmy November evening. The tropical breeze caressed us as we listened to a 60ish looking black male sing songs from the heart. Physically, he reminded me of the great blues and jazz singer, Joe Williams. His voice was smooth and soulful as his hands glided across the keyboard. He began the set with, "How Sweet It Is," a tune first made famous by Motown's Marvin Gaye and subsequently redone by singer, James Taylor. He closed with another Motown tune, "Ribbon in the Sky," by Stevie Wonder. It was the perfect finale.

I've always enjoyed listening to music outdoors and this particular evening was truly memorable. There were times when I believed the piano man was singing just for us. My delusion was not tainted by the fact that Louie's Backyard in Key West, Florida, had a full house. I enjoyed a glass of scotch, conch chowder and the music. It was hard to imagine life any sweeter.

Here I was on a warm evening in the company of my new bride, Lenora, enjoying fine dining and jamming to great music under the stars. It was late November. There wasn't a snowflake in sight – could it get any better than this?

Louie's Backyard is a well-known Key West hangout. It justifiably has a reputation for good food, music and ambiance. To top things off, Louie's directly faces the magical imaginary spot where the Atlantic Ocean and the Gulf of Mexico blend together. The result is a picturesque backdrop when having lunch or early dinner. The outdoor patio is surrounded by palms, sea grape trees and other colorful fauna. The vegetation and outdoor merriment helped to heighten the sense that we were in the tropics. As we held hands, Lenora and I stared into each others eyes. I said, "I guess we're not in Kansas anymore, Dorothy."

She asked, "Are you as happy as I am, Roger?"

I squeezed her hand, "Absolutely – this place is beautiful and we're not shoveling snow like we would be back home." The meteorologists were predicting eight to twelve inches of snow. Philly was already in the throes of a harsh early-winter freeze as we flew off to paradise.

When the set was wrapping up, the dapper-dressed singer announced, "My name is Bobalu and I hope you've enjoyed the show. If so, I hope you'll come back soon."

Before leaving Louie's that evening, we introduced ourselves to the crooner who had serenaded us.

"Did you like the music?"

"We did. Are you here every evening?"

"Yes!"

"Well, we'll be seeing you again."

The singer was 5' 11", brown and handsome.

As we walked through a passageway leading to our condo I asked, "Bobalu?" We laughed. It was a generational thing. One had to have lived in the sixties to get the joke. "Bobalu" – actually it was "Baba Looey," the sidekick of a cartoon character named QuickDraw McGraw. He was one of many creations by the team of Hanna Barbera seen on television back in the day. I could almost hear Fred Flintstone, another of their creations, shouting, "Wilma!"

Lenora and I knew that wasn't the piano man's real name, but it didn't matter. Soon we would learn that everyone living in Key West had a story. We enjoyed Bobalu's music and planned to see him perform again.

Bobalu had seen where we were heading and asked, "Are you folks staying at the Coconut Beach? That's a nice place. Have fun during your stay."

"That's the plan. So far so good." We walked through the door near Louie's outdoor bar to our romantic hideaway. Much would happen over the coming days and months, but nothing would alter how wonderful we felt that evening.

CHAPTER ONE

Petite with almond-brown skin, fifteen-year-old Mariela (pronounced Mary-Ella) Ramirez-James stood in Philadelphia's Juvenile Court, alongside her mother, Juanita and her bespeckled Attorney, Darlene Swift. Mariela was embarrassed and angry with herself. She had difficulty accepting the fact that she'd been arrested and was now standing in the honorable Jessie O'Brien's courtroom. What she had done had been stupid, but in her mind it was not a crime. Mariela kept hearing her mother's voice in her head. "Young lady, if a hundred people are about to jump off the Ben Franklin Bridge for the fun of it, would you join them?" Mariela's response had always been the same, "No, Ma! I'm not dumb or crazy." Juanita Ramirez, a fair-skinned middle-age single mother was a petite, attractive Cuban/African American woman. She replied, "We'll see."

Much to Mariela's regret, she had essentially taken the dreaded leap off that mythical bridge. Now it was time to pay the piper. Yes, she had exercised poor judgment. Two weeks before Thanksgiving, a few of her so-called girlfriends invited her to join them while they picked up a few things from Wanamaker's Department Store in downtown Philly. She accepted the offer. Mariela knew that her mother didn't approve of this crowd. But what harm could come from it? Mariela had heard about these five-finger discount shopping sprees, but she was no thief. She made it clear to her friends to count her out of that part of their plan. Mariela often felt isolated from her peers. They thought she was stuck up. She was rarely invited to join them and feared if she said no this time, they would never offer to socialize with her again. She wasn't stuck up – nor did she think she was better than anyone either. In truth, Mariela was lonely and just wanted to fit in. For once she would skip piano practice and do something fun. She really enjoyed playing the piano. Mariela could hear a song once and within minutes, play what she just heard on the piano. She had a gift. But sometimes, girls just want to have fun.

Mariela had been arrested with two other girls. Both of them were caught with unpaid store merchandise in their pockets. The price tags were still attached. Mariela was clean, but arrested anyway.

It would be a long time before she forgot how disappointed her mother looked when she arrived at the Juvenile Detention Center several weeks ago to get her out of custody. They didn't say a word to each other on the ride home. Although the ride itself was only thirty minutes, Mariela would have sworn it took several hours to get home that evening. Mariela now knew, beyond any reasonable doubt, that silence isn't always golden. In fact, Juanita's cold shoulder cut like a knife.

Eventually, mother and child did talk. Juanita spoke first, "Sometimes you remind me of your father. This is the kind of dumb crap that he'd do." Mariela remembered little about her dad, OJ, but the words hurt more than her mother would ever understand.

Judge O'Brien was still reviewing Mariela's file as the women awaited his decision. Judge O'Brien had the look of a boozer. His face was red, his eyes bloodshot and puffy. The man looked like he'd gone a few rounds with the bottle and lost. O'Brien had a reputation for being cold and uncaring. On top of that he was a pompous jerk. At the moment, his physical appearance was not relevant. All three women stood as erect as the Liberty Place Towers near 17th and Market Streets. Finally, O'Brien spoke. "Young lady, what you and your friends did was despicable. Everyone in society pays for goods when they're stolen from hard working merchants. The cost is passed on to all of us. Do you understand what I'm saying?"

Mariela meekly replied, "Yes, your honor."

"I don't suspect that you really do. You and your friends think this is no big deal, because it's a minor offense. I'm not impressed that this is your first arrest. Or that it's only a charge of shoplifting," he stated sarcastically. "What you did is a crime and I intend to make you think twice before you do something like that again."

Attorney Swift cleared her throat and attempted to interject.

"Your honor, we are all mindful that shoplifting is a crime but…"

Crusty Judge O'Brien looked sternly at Ms. Swift, "One moment, I'm not finished."

Looking like a female Harry Potter, Attorney Swift nodded, "Yes, your honor, I am sorry."

"The court sentences the accused to serve three months at the Children's Community Center."

Attorney Swift angrily said, "Your honor, three months at the Triple C for a first offense? With all due respect, that is extremely harsh."

Mariela and Juanita were both crying. Mariela mumbled "I didn't do anything."

Attorney Swift continued, "Your honor, this is unfair. You can't be serious."

"Ms. Swift, I am very serious. Our young people must learn that the law applies to everyone. If you don't like my sentence then file an appeal."

Swift retorted, "We certainly will – would the court entertain a stay until my appeal is heard?"

"No, Ms. Swift." Speaking to the court officer about Mariela, O'Brien said, "Take her away." Banging his gavel, "Court is now adjourned."

CHAPTER TWO

Key West, Florida is a place where locals and visitors celebrate every sunrise and sunset. It has a carnival atmosphere every day of the year. Most early risers don't even need an alarm clock. The neighborhood roosters start crowing early and often. It's as though they're shouting, "Hey folks, it's time to rise and get busy."

Lenora and I married in July but postponed our honeymoon until late fall. My new wife, Lenora, a Jimmy Buffett fan, had planned our arrival to coincide with the annual Parrothead Festival held at the Casa Marina Hotel. The Casa Marina was just around the corner from our condo at the Coconut Beach. Every few years, the singer himself would show up for the festival held in his honor. We were lucky Buffett was here and "Margaritaville" was alive, well and the joint was jumping.

The Festival provided adults of all ages and races the chance to listen to songs they'd heard millions of times and dress up in silly, outrageous costumes. Most wore headgear that looked like Macaws – hence the title "Parrotheads."

Lenora was in seventh heaven, dancing to the music and singing her heart out with the other crazy people attending the Festival. Who could begrudge hundreds of adults unwinding and reliving their teenage and college years for an evening?

This was a second marriage for both of us. Lenora's first husband, a military man, was a casualty in Operation Desert Storm. Lenora took his death very hard. Irene, my ex, divorced me seven years ago at my request. We had been law school sweethearts. At the time of our divorce, I was on death row in a Pennsylvania prison awaiting the needle. I'd been convicted of first-degree murder for killing my sister's paramour, Larry. Larry was my only niece Brandi's, biological father. Brandi and I are very close. It was Brandi's call for help that prompted me to go to Philly. Larry was being an ass and it scared her. I shot Larry in North Philly at the B&E Tavern. I'd come there to talk, but instead, I killed him in the heat of the moment. In death penalty cases, there is an automatic right to an appeal. My appellate lawyer, Frank, another law school classmate, discovered exculpatory evidence the police had not shared with my trial attorney. Frank learned that the police had recovered a gun that was in Larry's possession at the time of the shooting. Pennsylvania's Supreme Court reversed my murder conviction but offered the state the chance to try me again. The State Supreme Court concluded that I had the right to claim self-defense. Philly's District Attorney, at the time, had political aspirations. He feared the embarrassment of losing what had appeared to be a slam dunk. We cut a deal. I pled guilty to manslaughter and was sentenced to time served. I had been incarcerated for nearly four years at the time of my successful appeal. A condition of the agreement was that I surrender my license to practice law, no big deal since I lost my license when I was convicted. Fortunately, the Public Defender's Association in Philly needed a paralegal. Although I was over-qualified, I was grateful for the chance to work in the legal profession in some way.

Before my conviction, I had been very successful as a Baltimore trial lawyer. Irene and I were living quite comfortably prior to our divorce. We had a house in the city and one on Maryland's Eastern Shore. We were well on the path to becoming yuppies with a social conscience. My paternal grandmother, Sadie, had left me a solidly-built row house in North Philadelphia. It was paid for. All I had to do was pay the taxes. I didn't need to work. The divorce agreement left me with enough money to live comfortably for a while. But working was important to me. My inner voice told me that I had to atone. Working below my prior status seemed fair to me because I had taken the life of another human being. I had broken one of the sacred Ten Commandments – Thou Shall Not Kill. Whether I was justified under the law or not didn't absolve me of the heinous act. Larry needed killing. I just didn't have the right to be his executioner. Sure, he was a punk and bully – but I was a killer.

The managing attorney for the Defender's Association was Thom, also a law school buddy who helped me get set up in the new job. My work with the Defender's Association had proven helpful for both Thom and me.

Together, we secured justice where otherwise innocent, truly innocent people, would have been in prison.

Lenora and I met on a blind date arranged by Brandi, Lenora's co-worker. One thing I can say for my niece is that I admire her taste in friends. After a courtship of a year, Lenora and I married in an open-air ceremony last July in Rittenhouse Square. By then, my first wife, Irene had found a new partner and they attended our wedding service. We were friends, but as B.B. King sings, "The thrill was gone." It was long gone.

Lenora and I flew out of Philly the second week in November for two weeks of sun and fun in Key West. I had never been there but Lenora promised me, "Roger, you'll love it." So off we went on our delayed honeymoon. When we departed, the temperature was twenty-five degrees. After a brief layover in Tampa, USAir deposited us in Key West, Florida. When I stepped off the plane, the sky was crystal blue and the temperature a warm and cozy seventy-six degrees. We landed about two-thirty in the afternoon. Immediately, my shoulders began to relax and I was ready to play. Lenora pointed out that according to her friend, Anne, "Key West is the adult version of Disneyland. It's a combination of New Orleans and Las Vegas." Anne was right. Lenora took care of all of our arrangements. Anne suggested the Coconut Beach Resort because it was adjacent to the Casa Marina and within walking distance of almost everything else worth seeing or doing on the island, including the Southernmost Point.

The Coconut Beach Resort is a private tropical paradise situated on the serene Atlantic Ocean. Its condominiums are a blend of old Key West architecture, lush vegetation and quiet walkways flowing onto bright verandas. There's an oceanfront pool and jacuzzi. For those who desire the real thing, there's a sandy beach to dip their toes into the Atlantic. The verandas are dotted with old-fashioned rocking chairs that enhance the sense that the resort is a place to leave one's troubles behind and enjoy the water and sun. The place is also an ideal spot to catch a spectacular Key West sunset.

Our unit had two bedrooms, a kitchen and two baths. The really special part, however, was the wraparound veranda. We had an unobstructed view of the daily sunsets. The area is called the Southernmost Point because this part of the Florida Keys is a mere ninety miles from Cuba. It is also the Southernmost Point of the Continental USA. Anne and Lenora made the perfect choice for our two-week getaway.

Lenora failed to mention that the Parrothead Festival began on the second evening of our stay. But in truth, I didn't care. She was happy and I was happy for her. Lenora whispered in my ear in between songs, "Roger, you'll get your reward in trade later for being such a good sport." She said it in such a seductive tone that visions of more than sugar plums danced in my head.

CHAPTER THREE

On our third day, we walked down to the multicolored buoy that boldly proclaimed, "Southernmost Point of the USA." The buoy was painted in yellow, black, and blue surrounded by white bands. According to locals, there used to be simple signs, "Southernmost Point" but rambunctious partiers kept stealing them. A concrete buoy labeled Southernmost Point was erected and the mischief came to an end. As we meandered along Whitehead Street, you could tell that ordinary folks lived here. Our stroll on Whitehead eventually brought us to President Harry Truman's White House. From there, it was only a short walk to Mallory Square. At Mallory's, you find street performers and others who come together to celebrate the start of sunset. Sword swallowers, jugglers, fire eaters, musicians and pirates, "Arrgh," gather with locals and tourists to say farewell to daylight and usher in the evening. Evenings in Key West are filled with good food, music and all other forms of debauchery. We would eventually take in the happenings at Mallory but the Truman White House was our first destination.

During his Presidency, Truman frequently visited Key West. The mini White House was situated on a naval base. The house was large enough to accommodate Mr. Truman's entourage of family, cronies and Secret Service. The President often played cards on the porch. Since the house is still a functioning government building and museum, much of it was left exactly as it was during the Truman era. This included the President's secretary quarters, card table, Presidential desk, bedroom and bar. Truman signed Executive Order 9981 there on July 26, 1948. Order 9981 desegregated the Armed Forces.

The Museum at the White House contained copies of the infamous Chicago Tribune Newspaper. In bold type, it proclaimed "Dewey Wins" the 1948 Presidential race. There were numerous photos of President Truman holding a copy of the newspaper with what can best be described as a "shit eating" grin. His smile ran from ear to ear. In a careful review of the paper you could tell that in addition to getting the facts wrong, the Trib had other errors in that special edition. We learned that the Trib was in the midst of a labor dispute and the typesetting had been done by members of management. Apparently it was amateur night at the Tribune that evening. In addition to getting the story wrong, the typesetting was disjointed and in some cases, the text was even backwards.

Standing in the spot where Executive Order 9981 was issued was particularly poignant to me. My Dad, "Big Roger" was in the service during that time. He had a very distinct recollection of that day. "Son, it was like someone had suddenly turned on the lights after years of darkness. Where I was stationed, segregation ended immediately. Some General stopped the movie we had been watching and the black soldiers were ordered to come down from the balcony and sit downstairs. For decades, only the white soldiers were permitted to sit in the good seats." Clearly, Big Roger saw this as an important moment in history.

From Truman's White House we walked about a half block to Kelly's, where we had a late lunch. It was Happy Hour – two margaritas for five dollars. The food was fine but the drinks were great. The actress, Kelly McGillis, owns the restaurant. I first remembered seeing her in the murder/mystery film, "Witness." She co-starred with Harrison Ford and Danny Glover. Kelly's is a landmark of sorts. It's situated in the middle of a commercial district and just a few steps from Mallory Square.

Lenora and I had heard so much about Mallory Square that we decided to stay for sunset. As we had been forewarned, there was a carnival atmosphere. Street performers, pirates and wenches, "Arrgh" lined the streets. People gathered; everyone seemed happy. They were anticipating a special event. As the sun began to fade, people stood in silent awe. Then they clapped and cheered. The festiveness of the moment was contagious. We slowly walked away knowing that tomorrow would bring more of the same. By the time we strolled back to the Coconut Beach, neither of us was really hungry, so we stopped for cocktails and appetizers at Louie's. While there, we first met and heard dapper Bobalu perform. We listened, enchanted by the tone of his voice and exquisite selection of music. After listening to Jimmy Buffet the day before, Bobalu's R&B was literally music to my ears. At the end of the set, we exchanged pleasantries with the artist and pledged that we'd be back again.

As we slipped through the door by the outside bar to the grounds of the Coconut Beach, we overheard someone talking about the Casa Marina hosting a fashion show for pets the following afternoon. At Lenora's insistence, we decided to catch the show. The next morning we hung around our pool area and enjoyed the sun. Later, armed with cocktails, we walked across the street to see the show. The fashion show was an annual benefit for the Lower Keys Friends of Animals. I've often questioned whether pets really take on the affect of their owners. The fashion show demonstrated that the answer to that question was unequivocally yes. The overall winner was a sloth and his/her owner. The owner was dressed like a tree and the sloth just hung there in a burst of true slothiness. It was all silly but harmless fun. Lenora was just a chatterbox. "Did you see the dog or wasn't that cat cute?" I mumbled something appropriate as we retired to our living quarters.

Over the remainder of our stay in Key West we fell into a routine. Breakfast was either in our condo or at Camille's. Camille's is Key West at its funky best. The food is always great and the décor interesting, to say the least. One side of the establishment is lined with naughty Barbie dolls clad in black lingerie and posed in positions that Mattel never considered. I was particularly fond of dominatrix Barbie. She was the least sexually provocative of the group. We also enjoyed the ceramic blue and pink coitus standing hogs. I was surprised that we ever managed to actually eat because everywhere we gazed something new caught our attention. After breakfast, we'd return to our pool area to bask in the sun and contemplate our activities for the remainder of the day. By now, our evenings were already set in stone. We always ended with a cocktail at Louie's as we listened to the soulful sounds of Bobalu.

One evening, we dined at "Blue Heaven." This eatery had great food and an interesting history. It was said that Ernest "Papa" Hemingway bet on cock fights and participated in bare knuckle fist fighting there when he wasn't using the brothel upstairs. The restaurant has a saying, "you don't have to die to get to heaven." Our meal was indeed heavenly. Our server, Robin, was perhaps the most knowledgeable person we met during our stay in Key West. Robin took the time to school us on the do's and don'ts in Key West.

Lenora and I both declined dessert although the Key Lime pie tested our resolve. But we held firm. Our strength had little to do with counting calories. While walking down Petronia Street to Blue Heaven, we passed a dessert shop that aroused our curiosity.

The name itself made it impossible for us to resist. It was called "Better than Sex" and its owners were the Master Bakers. The menu included tasty delights such as Kelly's Klimax, Jaclyn's Gyration, Carmel Over Me, Adult Apple, Sex Appeal, Tongue Bath Truffle, Missionary Crisp, Between My Red Velvet Sheets Cheese Cake, Seven Year Itch and Jungle Fever. I chose the "Tongue Bath Truffle" and Lenora tore into "Kelly's Klimax." Virtually, all the dishes contained a little chocolate for obvious reasons. Our desserts were not better than sex but a close second. Lenora did her best Meg Ryan imitation from "When Harry Met Sally." She noisily devoured her dessert, and had the bad taste to loudly sigh afterwards. Along with everyone in the restaurant, I laughed so hard my hair hurt which is impossible since my head had been shaved for eight years. People applauded as we walked out and headed back down Duval Street towards the Coconut Beach.

While walking towards Louie's we heard, "*Who can say – what brought us this miracle we've found – there are those who bet –love comes but once and yet – I'm so glad we met the second time around.*" The Sammy Kahn song, "*The Second Time Around*" made famous by Frank Sinatra, seemed to have been written just for us.

When we entered Louie's, Bobalu was between sets. I asked him, "So, are you a native conch, or a transplant?" Key Westers refer to themselves as "Conchs." When Key West was first settled, conch and conch shells were so plentiful that these shells were ground and mixed into a substance that was used like bricks to build homes. They were called conch houses. The roofs were galvanized steel. The ceilings were open and high enough that the houses were naturally air conditioned. The conch, or clam, itself made a fine meal.

"No, I grew up in Philadelphia, PA."

"Really? That's where we're from. I'm a paralegal and Lenora works in MIS at Drexel University."

"That sounds interesting."

Lenora pointed out, "Being a musician is far more interesting than what either of us do for a living."

"What part of Philly, Bobalu?"

"Back in 1963 I lived in West Philly. I'd just graduated from West Catholic High School. By 1964 I was in Nam. I was a week from entering Haverford College when Uncle Sam ordered me to Southeast Asia."

"Wow! I mean." Stumbling for the right words, "Oh, man, that was a tough break," I said. "You just missed qualifying for a student deferment by a week. That is cold."

"You have no idea, Roger. Many of my buddies came back in tough shape and I was no exception. By the end of 1967 I was discharged, strung out and home for good. I was useless. The next decade was a blur – I was wasted. But I had learned how to play a variety of instruments while in high school and was a weekend Julliard student as a teenager. I'd still be strung out and useless but in 1981 my mom got sick and died. I could see the pain and disappointment in her eyes. After she was buried, I checked into a VA hospital. It took a little time but by the mid-eighties I had things together."

"Hey, music was hot in Philly at that time. Gamble and Huff were churning out hit songs faster than the US Mint prints money. I assume it was a good time for you to be a musician?"

"You're right. There was a lot of studio work for a guy with my training and I took advantage of the opportunity. There were lots of gigs with a few well-known artists and lots of wannabes. Listen, I've got to get back to work. Are you staying for the next set?"

Lenora noted, "We wouldn't miss it – go for it, piano man."

Bobalu nodded and smiled as he tiptoed back to his keyboard.

The set began with Bobalu singing the Carole King song, "*Will You Still Love Me Tomorrow*?" He closed out with a tune by Philly's own Stylistics, "*You Are Everything*." To me, it was great to see that Bobalu had not forgotten his Philadelphia roots.

After completing his set, Lenora and I invited him to join us for a nightcap. "Thanks, but I'll just have a ginger ale if you don't mind? I haven't had a drink in fifteen years."

I said, "Congratulations! Not many of us are able to beat back our demons."

"It isn't easy. Every day is a struggle. But the choices for me are life or drink." For a moment, we all sat quietly.

"How did you end up in Key West?"

"I became an official resident of the Conch Republic in the winter of 2001. The annual battles with the cold, the Hawk and Jack Frost were kicking my butt. Besides, I was concerned that I'd slip back into my trifling ways – drinking, drugs, you know the whole scene."

So I asked, "If you were afraid of backsliding, then why here?"

"Like I said, I needed a change in climate and scenery. I don't miss the cold. As for all the crazy and foolish stuff that goes on here, for some strange reason, I'm not tempted. Maybe it's because I see how dumb people act when they're drinking. I'm just so turned off by the whole scene that I'm not interested."

"If it's okay for you, I'm in no position to judge."

"I can say that, as odd as it all seems, it works for me."

"Well, we're happy for you. Do you still have family and friends in Philly?"

"Yeah." He paused and for a moment things felt uncomfortable. It was as if Bobalu wanted to say more but couldn't right then.

"Listen, I don't mean to be so dramatic. It's been great talkin' with you but I need my beauty sleep."

He laughed and so did we. The moment passed.

"Go on, we understand – we're newlyweds on vacation. I believe it's against the rules for us to sleep. We live for the sunrises and sunsets. Goodnight and we'll see you tomorrow."

After he left, Lenora asked, "Did we say something wrong?"

"Who knows honey? Maybe the guy was just tired. Speaking of which, didn't you promise me payment in trade for sitting through the Parrothead Festival the other day?"

Lenora smiled as though she was shocked by what I just said.

"Roger, I swear those years in prison turned you into a satyriasis."

"What is that term you ladies throw around at Drexel when you talk about men? I prefer that you call me your "love machine" and baby I'm all yours. Let's go – before you know it, those damn roosters will start crowing."

We walked off hand in hand under a lovely crescent moon.

CHAPTER FOUR

The next day, Lenora tried parasailing. I passed on the opportunity, but watched her gracefully ascend. It was an amazing sight. I love her sense of adventure. To be truthful I am envious. Up in the sky Lenora reminded me of an angel in flight.

Once my angel returned to earth, the devil in her took over. Lenora kept making clucking sounds implying that I was a chicken. We bicycled back from parasailing to the Coconut Beach. I jumped into the hot tub/spa. Lenora took a swim in the pool. We returned to our little spot around the pool area and began reading our respective books.

Don Dee – a fellow everyone calls the "Mayor" of Coconut Beach came over for a chat. Don is a retiree. He and his wife are regulars at the resort. Don's a talker – but he's a sweet and funny guy. As best we can tell, the man is always smiling. Don dodged a major heart attack years ago. He said to me, "Hey, fella, I smile all the time because I'm thankful for every day." We agreed with him. Then he started teasing us. He started gesturing with his hands, "I can always tell the newlyweds. How long? What, six months?"

"How'd you know?"

"You both have the glow – the trick is to keep it after thirty years."

We promised that we would and that if it ever started to fade "we'll call you."

Don pointed a finger at his chest, "You do that – keep it fresh and alive."

* * *

"Hon, isn't this the life?"

Lenora said, "Yes it is. Would you like to try Sarabeth's tonight?"

"Sure, what the hell."

"Roger, there's a Sarabeth's in New York City on the Upper Eastside. They serve amazing breakfasts and their pastries are to die for. I wonder if they're related." Sarabeth's is located on the corner of Simonton and Southard Streets. The building used to be a synagogue. Sarabeth's has an outdoor terrace, surrounded by a white picket fence. We chose to dine under the stars. Sarabeth's is a place where down-home cooking meets nouveau cuisine. You can get old fashioned fried chicken or lump crabmeat with cornmeal crusted Key West shrimp cakes with jicama, mango and pineapple slaw.

Lenora began with Sarabeth's velvety cream of tomato soup. She had fresh filet of salmon, sautéed with fresh herbs and served with an orzo and vegetable salad. I tried the fried chicken. It was good. I wondered if someone had stolen Grandma Sadie's recipe. We shared dessert. Stuffed to the gills, we walked, or should I say, waddled, back to the Coconut Beach. The long walk back was good exercise.

We were back at Louie's in time for Bobalu's first set. He waved to us and then launched into his rendition of "*It Was Just My Imagination,*" one of Lenora's favorite songs. From that song, the tunes continued to flow like fine wine. We loved every minute of it.

At the end of his set, Bobalu came over to us. "I want to apologize to you guys."

In unison we asked, "Why?"

"Last night you asked me about Philly and family. I dodged the question – I was embarrassed."

Lenora said gently, "You don't owe us an explanation. If we crossed some line, we're both very sorry."

"No, no! You've got it wrong. If you guys can hang around until the end of my next set, I'll explain."

"Sure, we'll be here – but before you go what's your real name?"

"Oscar James – OJ!" Bobalu rolled his eyes and said, "I'll see you once I finish my set."

He began this time with the Beatles' tune "*Yesterday*." He was so soulful that both of us teared up a bit.

When Bobalu finished, he brought over his ginger ale and joined us.

"So, what did you guys think of the set?"

"Oh man you were really kickin it – it was good. You should think about recording that '*Yesterday*' number. It's really special."

"Thanks!"

"As I mentioned last night, it took some time for me to find myself. At sixty, I'm a baby-daddy of sorts. I have a little girl back in Philly and I haven't seen her or her mother Juanita since I came to Key West. Mariela should be about fifteen now and it's time for me to make things right."

"How are you gonna do that?" I asked.

Bobalu got a serious look on his face, "Roger, Lenora, I need a favor. I've been setting aside money every week for my little girl since I arrived here. I'm sure that she and her mother could use the money. I've got twenty thousand dollars saved for my little girl."

When he said that I was very uncool and coughed up a little of my drink. "Sorry!"

"That's understandable. By the way I prefer Bobalu to OJ. I've had enough troubles in my life. I don't need to carry around Mr. Simpson's baggage too – even if it's only a joke."

"We both understand."

Anyway, here's the last picture I have of Mariela. She was seven or eight when it was taken.

Lenore looked at the picture, "She's beautiful."

"Thank you! She gets her looks from her mother."

Lenore said, "Not all of them. She has your eyes."

"When I left Philadelphia they lived in Mount Airy. I have an address but I don't know if it's still good. I can't go back there for a number of reasons. There are outstanding non-support warrants and some things we've talked about already. But I love my kid and I want her to have this money. Maybe she'll even want to come and see me down here in a few years. This money is just a start. Would you guys do me a huge favor and give this check to Mariela and Juanita for me?"

We were both speechless. Finally I asked, "Oscar, are you sure you want us to do this for you? I mean, we're essentially strangers to you."

"Absolutely, I've met a lot of couples from Philly over the years but you two are the first that I've felt comfortable talking with about this thing. Please, you'd do me the honor?"

"Can we think about it overnight?"

"Sure, you'd be crazy if you didn't. I understand completely. I can't begin to tell you just how much I appreciate you even considering the idea."

"Okay. We'll let you know tomorrow."

"Thanks! Thank you so much. Now that I've gotten that off my chest, can I change the subject?"

"Sure"

"I know you guys love music – particularly 'old school'." He smiled, "By any chance, have you heard the music of a singer named Bessie Smith?"

"Sure, who hasn't?"

"Not that one. There was a woman – an old woman now, who lived in the Strawberry Mansion area of North Philly around 33rd Street. She was a part blues/part jazz singer. She was Philly's version of Lady Day – Billie Holiday, without the drugs and drama. Man, this woman was a legend. She could bring down the house when she sang, '*God Bless the Child*' or '*Someone to Watch Over Me'*. When I was learning about music, people still talked about this woman and her sidekick. By then no one could recall having heard her sing in years. But those who had heard Miss Smith, talked about her talent with a reverence usually reserved for the true greats. This woman had pipes."

Lenore and I looked at each other. "Roger has a neighbor by the same name. She was his grandmother, Sadie's, best friend."

"Really? That's interesting. Is she about 80? You guys said how much you enjoyed my version of '*Yesterday*'. I'm told that Ms. Bessie could take pretty much any ballad and with her voice and style, she'd make grown men and women cry like babies. Roger, did she just say that your grandmother's name was Sadie?"

"Yes! But I know nothing about … why are you asking?"

"Man, Miss Bessie would have this woman named Sadie on stage with her sometimes. They'd do a duet – but mostly it was Bessie. When I was growing up, I looked far and wide for a recording by these divas. I found one recording. The quality was poor, but her singing and Sadie's … Oh man, you wouldn't believe what a great sound they had. That Bessie's voice was so powerful, I felt like she was in the room when I listened to the recording. She was BAD."

Lenora and I were both stunned. I had no idea our elderly neighbor, Bessie, had been a great vocalist. And Grandma Sadie? Who would have thought!

Lenora and I had puzzled looks on our faces. Bobalu was laughing his ass off, having fun at our expense. "Shoot, man, you had no idea about the level of talent that surrounded you. I bet you just saw them as church ladies. That's so funny. But you know, it's typical of many of the old folks from back in the day. They didn't brag or wallow in what they used be. We could all learn something from them." Again he laughed – "Poor Roger living near two of the hottest singers of their generation and knowing nothing about it. Well, I guess they had their reasons. When you get back to Philly please, pretty please, give Miss Bessie my regards. I'm a fan from way back. You know, Roger, I'm just having a little fun with you now. But if your Miss Bessie and Grandmother Sadie aren't the two that I have in mind, then Secretariat didn't win the Triple Crown. Don't be sad, my friend. Rejoice! You lived with musical royalty."

"You're probably right about all of this Bobalu, I'm just in shock."

"I understand. Let me bid you folks a good night. Don't keep him up to late, Lenora." Lenora blushed. "Please give my request some consideration and we'll talk tomorrow. Good night!"

Lenora and I, still stunned by the revelation about Bessie and Grandma Sadie, just stared at the stars in wonder. "Holy Shit," I said. "Babe, this is some weird stuff."

"Roger, let's not jump to conclusions, but if this is all true, then what a great story."

"Honey, you're right. Come on. Let's call it a night."

She looked at me, “Are we going to sleep or are you planning to keep me up until sunrise again?”

“I don’t recall you protesting last night.”

“No, I didn’t. Let’s go.”

CHAPTER FIVE

We spent another day sightseeing and looking at jewelry and other creations by local artists. For lunch we stopped at the "Turtle Kraal." The Turtle Kraal has a distinct natural feel. It's situated on the Historic Seaport of Key West. The shack-like structure with a covered patio and open air view sits on a pier just above the Gulf of Mexico. You can have meals anytime of the day while watching fishing boats and leisure crafts pull into their berths. Known best for seafood, you can also get excellent BBQ. From a merchandizing standpoint, the Kraal sells license plates which read "Half Raw Bar, Eat it Raw, Key West, FL."

As we were being directed to our table, I noticed a fella seated at the bar that looked vaguely familiar to me. Lenora grabbed my arm, "Roger, stop staring at people. It's rude." While we were eating, the stranger came up to us.

"Excuse me, but you wouldn't by chance be Roger Work?"

"Yes sir, I think that I know you, too, but I can't say why."

"Hot damn – Criminal Law, Roger – law school."

"Professor Russ?"

"The one and only."

"How long has it been, sir – nearly thirty years?"

"That sounds about right. I'm sorry Miss, I taught this guy and his motley crew Criminal Law when they were first-year students. My name is Russ. What's yours?"

"Lenora. Roger and I are here on our honeymoon."

"Congratulations to both of you. Roger you old dog, how did you manage to convince such a young, charming and attractive woman to marry you?"

"Just dumb luck, I guess. What brings you to Key West?"

"I moved here. After I retired, I bought a fishing boat and now I captain fishing tours."

"Wow, that's some career change."

"Yeah, but I love it. Are you still in touch with the members of your little law school clique? Irene, Joyce, Thom and Frank, I believe those were the names?"

"Man, you're amazing. First of all, to remember me and then my friends, too. Yes, we're all still tight."

"That's great to hear. Your class was a special one. I'll never forget any of you. Listen, I won't take up anymore of your time but if you and your bride would like to see the island from the water, just give me a call. I'm in the book. I'd love to take you out and catch up on old times."

"Thanks, Russ. We'll give that some thought. It's great to see you."

* * *

"Well, that was some surprise Roger."

"It sure was. Let's head back to the Coconut Beach. I have a massage scheduled for 2:30."

For supper, we dined at La Te Da's on Duval Street. I had meatloaf. After eating lots of exotic dishes for over a week I wanted a little comfort food. The meatloaf hit the spot. Lenora had Red Snapper. The restaurant is located in one of many Inns – (bed and breakfasts) that you find in Key West. With their unique design and ambiance, these places add to the rich color of Key West.

Later in the evening, we met with Bobalu at Louie's. Earlier in the day, we agreed to deliver the package to his daughter. When we told Bobalu, he said, "Thanks. You have no idea how good that makes me feel." We shared with him that we'd be departing Key West in two days. Bobalu promised to get us the check and contact information the next day.

To our surprise, at the start of the set, Bobalu told the audience that, "These first two numbers are for a lovely couple here from Philadelphia, my hometown." Then he launched into "*Misty*" and "*Hello Young Lovers*." We were both touched by his kindness in addition to loving the music.

As promised, we met with Bobalu the next day. With check and info in hand, we bid him farewell. "You'll get progress reports every week." Early the following morning, we headed back to Philly. We were looking forward to celebrating our first Christmas as a married couple. I was also anxious to learn more about Miss Bessie and my Grandmother, Sadie.

CHAPTER SIX

It didn't take long for the chill of winter to settle into my bones once we exited Philadelphia's International Airport. We enjoyed our Key West vacation but all good things eventually come to an end. Besides the cold, the partially snow covered ground was a grim reminder that we were home.

Thanksgiving was just days away. Brandi was hosting this year. Because the holiday was late this year, store merchants were already complaining about the shorter shopping season.

Since it was a Sunday evening, we decided to stay at Lenora's house. Both of us were expected at work first thing in the morning. By staying in Center City, we both could get to our respective offices without driving or relying on public transportation.

During our vacation, we had failed to resolve the issue of whether our primary residence would be Lenora's house, which was effectively downtown Philly, or my place on 33rd Street in North Philly. At the moment, we were too tired to worry about our riches in housing.

After unpacking and taking a quick shower, we went to bed. Lenora mentioned something like, "Roger, if you touch me other than to kiss me good night, I'll strangle you." Coward that I am, I readily acquiesced to her threat of imminent bodily harm. In the morning we rushed around getting dressed. Breakfast was light. Our cupboard was bare. We needed to do some food shopping asap. As we were leaving the house, Lenora reminded me to start looking for Mariela.

When I arrived at the office, Thom, my friend and boss, commented on my beautiful tan. I slipped my wedding ring off my third finger. The skin tone was lighter than the rest of my hand. I gave him a good natured, Bronx salute to help illustrate the point. "See, wise ass. I missed you, too. So, do you have anything special for me?"

"There are some matters on your desk but nothing urgent. I hope you remembered Malik will start his winter recess right after Thanksgiving, so you'll need to keep him busy." Malik was a neighborhood friend and best man at our wedding. He was in his junior year at Lincoln University.

When I first met Malik, he was dealing drugs on a street corner in North Philly. Drug traffic on our streets had been and continues to be a problem. But there was something about Malik. He seemed familiar to me. Malik lacked the swagger of some of the other street dealers in the neighborhood. I decided to take a chance. I attempted to befriend him. Once we started talking, in spite of our difference in age, nearly thirty years, we found common ground. Malik and I had gone to the same high school. We also had the same mentor. After a rough patch, I found him a job with the Defender's Association.

My mind had wandered. Turning to Thom, "Don't worry big guy, I've got it covered. What about the armed bank robbery case that came in just before vacation?"

"Our client, Darren Young, was arrested and charged with the bank robbery after the police got his name from an informant. Witnesses at the crime scene told officers that a person wearing a costume came into the bank around eleven in the morning. The getup alone got everyone's attention. But just to be sure, the alleged perp discharged one shot into the ceiling before demanding that the clerks empty their cash trays into his bag." Thom continued, "It'll be interesting. The prosecutor's office is planning to use FBI experts to link Mr. Young to the getaway car and glock supposedly used during the crime. There are no clear photos of the bank robber. The robber wore a Philly Phanatic costume. It covered his entire body." The Philly Phanatic is the mascot for the Philadelphia Phillies baseball club. The green fur outfit runs from head to toe. The creature has a long snout, a pot belly and wears sneakers. Thom continued "without the informant, the cops would have nothing on our client. But the informant acknowledges driving the getaway car for Mr. Young. You'll love this part. The informant claims that this was all Young's idea. Our client supplied a stolen car, the gun and the costume. Young is alleged to have stolen the car the evening prior to the stick-up. Hence, the fingerprint. Did I mention that the informant had been busted with a pound of heroin? In exchange for pleading guilty to driving the car, the government will drop the drug charge."

"Has discovery started yet?"

"Oh yeah. Fingerprints lifted from the car and the ballistics report on the gun were delivered last Friday. Our client swears that he's innocent and is demanding a speedy trial. So, you probably should start by going over the lab reports. Young acknowledged being in the car but he didn't know it was stolen. A friend offered him a ride to work so he accepted the invitation. Mr. Young has no priors and he's afraid he'll lose his job if this drags on too long."

"Okay, Chief, I'll get right on it."

As I worked my way through the piles of mail and information from the Prosecutor's Office, I began to feel overwhelmed. This always happened at the start of a new case. There were a few strands that could prove promising, however. When I looked up, I realized it was lunchtime. It didn't seem right to use office time, so I used my lunch time to begin my search for Mariela. I began to explore some of the database systems available to our office to see if I could find anything on Juanita or Mariela Ramirez. I was not entirely surprised when I came up with nothing. Mariela was too young to drive or vote. I had a fifty percent chance of locating either using driving records. I had hoped that Juanita's name might appear on the voter registration rolls. But I struck out there, too. Now, it was apparent that my search would require a little more effort than I had assumed. The good news was that neither woman's names appeared in any of our criminal data systems. Interestingly enough, Oscar's (Bobalu's) name was listed as a deadbeat dad. The amount that he had given us more than covered his outstanding debt. But his instinct not to come to Philly himself was a good decision. Once things were cleared up, he would be able to return home without fear of arrest.

After my lunch hour and database searches were completed, I called Lenora to see how she was doing on her first day back to work. We also discussed the lack of information on Juanita and Mariela.

"I love you and I'll see you around six."

"Me too," said Lenora.

In the stack of mail on my desk, I found a magazine, ***Recent Developments in Forensics***. In bold type, the headline on the cover was a story suggesting that both fingerprint evidence and ballistic testing were unreliable forms of proof. The author, a former FBI special agent, had worked in the fingerprint, ballistic and fiber areas of the Bureau. He asserted this sort of evidence should rarely be admissible at trial and never as a basis of establishing identification. "Very interesting!" I said to no one in particular. The remainder of my day whizzed by and before I knew it, it was quitting time. I passed by Thom as I was leaving the office. "Are you and Richard joining us for Thanksgiving this year? It's Brandi's turn to host but you guys have a standing invitation."

"I'll let you know in the morning – if that's okay?"

"Sure!"

Thom and I were law school classmates and pals. He transferred from Delaware School of Law to Temple Law School after his first year because of family issues. At the time no one knew that Thom was gay. After I was released from prison, we had a conversation and he told me his secret. When we were in law school very few people admitted to being gay. They suffered in silence. It was not easy for Thom to trust me. But I felt honored. Soon Thom and his partner, Richard, became two of my closest friends.

By the time I got home Lenora had done some shopping and had supper ready. I am married to Wonder Woman. "Thanks honey. I should have been more thoughtful."

"No problem, it's your turn tomorrow."

While eating Lenora asked, "Did you call Brandi to see what she wants us to bring for Thanksgiving?"

"No, I forgot. Besides since you both work in the same office, I figured you'd talk about Thursday's menu."

"Hey, buster, you're the cook – you better call her!"

"Okay! I'll call now."

Once the conversation was over it was decided. Lenora was to prepare macaroni and cheese, I would bake bread, a few desserts and a Southwestern style roast beef. Lenora and I would also pick up Ms. Bessie.

We were both exhausted and retired by 10:00 o'clock. This time there were no overt threats.

* * *

I arrived at the office around 8:30 AM. Our receptionist/paralegal, Angela, advised me that Thom would be in court all day. Since Angela had lived in Philly all of her life, I asked, "Are you familiar with the Mount Airy area?"

"I've been up there a few times. When people started leaving North Philly while I was growing up lots of them moved there. Mount Airy is still technically part of the city. But folks believed that streets were safer and the schools were better. I've got a cousin who lives there. She seems happy and she's got a nice house."

"Great, maybe you can give me some directions and advice. I need to find a young lady and her mother." Then I went on to tell her about the odd favor we'd been asked to perform while on vacation.

"That's nice of you guys. I'll help if I can."

"Thanks, Angela. Let me get back to my sweat shop." She laughed.

"Oh, Roger, Malik called. He said he'll be in the office on Monday morning."

"Thanks, I'll start to get some work lined up for him."

"I really like Malik. I think he'll be a great lawyer some day."

"Me, too."

I returned to my office to do some work. After reading the forensic science magazine, I began to think that Thom might want to file a '*Daubert* motion' to have the fingerprint and ballistic evidence recovered by the police excluded from trial. Under *Daubert,* scientific evidence is not admissible at trial unless it is both relevant and reliable. Thom, during his motion, would attempt to convince the judge that the fingerprint and ballistic evidence is not the product of reliable science. In fact if the publishers of the magazine were correct, there is no underlying valid scientific principle for any of the evidence in question. Because the science is not reliable, it cannot be considered as evidence. Assuming the forensic magazine was correct, Thom would win on his motion. A successful motion would gut the government's entire case.

I would need to become more familiar with the science and then see if we could find credible experts to take on the FBI witnesses likely to be used.

There was a small part of me that quietly hoped that we would not prevail in our *Daubert* motion. If we were correct, then hundreds, if not thousands of people had been wrongfully convicted over the years. Some people may have even been executed. What a nightmare. But our job was to take this one step at a time and do the best possible job we could.

Around 11 o'clock I telephoned Ms. Bessie.

"Hello, Roger, is that you?"

"Yes, ma'am. Lenora and I are back in town. We were wondering if you'd be joining us for Thanksgiving. It will be the usual crowd except that Lenora's sister, Liz, will be joining our motley crew. You met Liz at the wedding in July."

"Child, you know how much I love spending time with you all."

"Yes Ma'am, we feel the same way about you. Brandi is hosting dinner this year. Can Lenora and I pick you up around 3 o'clock on Thursday?"

"That will be just fine. How was Florida?"

"Very nice. It was great to spend two weeks with temperatures in the mid to high seventies. By the way did JT or Third make sure that your walkway was shoveled while we were away?"

"They sure did. You know those friends of yours have always been gentlemen."

"Good, I'm glad to hear they took care of business. If they hadn't we wouldn't let them have a second helping on Thursday."

"Oh Roger, stop your fooling around."

"Miss Bessie while we were in Key West we met a fan of yours."

"Honey, what are you talkin' about?"

"We were told that you used to be a famous singer – in fact Grandma Sadie was supposed to have worked with you at times."

"Roger, who told you that?"

"Like I said, a fan."

"Humph! Roger I'll see you on Thursday, I'll make a pot of collards mixed with cabbage."

"I was hoping you would. We'll see you then. If you need anything, you know how to reach us."

"Okay, see you on Thursday, child."

I heard the dial tone. The conversation was over. Ms. Bessie had neither confirmed nor denied the story. I decided it would take a little finesse to get the story behind the story. Then I started laughing. What if OJ was right?

You can never tell about people. Miss Bessie had been part of my life since the day I was born. She and grandma had been friends since grammar school.

I've seen old pictures of them. The photo's probably date back to the fifties. They were both attractive. Each had a glimmer of mischief in their eyes. Back then, women weren't supposed to look like twigs or lollipops. These women had some meat on their bones. Grandpa Work had somethin' to wrap his arms around. "The girls," as they used to refer to themselves, did everything together. They married about the same time and even bought their homes on the same street.

After grandpa's death, Miss Bessie made an extra effort to keep an eye on Sadie. When Grandma Sadie passed, Bessie was at her bedside. Since my release from prison, Miss Bessie has been my guardian angel. As I reflect on things, when Bessie got Malik and me out of a real jam several years ago, it should have been clear that she was one of a kind. It's still hard for me to believe that almost five years ago, she shot JT's brother, Eric, a major drug dealer who was about to kill us. We had figured out that he was the one bringing illegal drugs into our neighborhood. When Eric discovered we knew his secret, he lured us to the basement of a vacant house. Eric's plan included driving us to a deserted part of Fairmont Park where he would shoot Malik and me leaving our bodies to rot. As we were getting into his car parked in the alleyway, eighty-something-year-old Miss Bessie appeared with a gun in her hand. She asked, "Eric, what are you doin? "

"Old woman, mind your own business."

Noticing that Eric had a gun, in a scene out of "Gunsmoke" or some cowboy TV show, she shot Eric in the arm. He dropped the gun and then started crying like a baby.

"Eric, it's time you moved away. Go out West. I don't care where, but get out of our neighborhood. If you don't, I'll take care of you. Do you understand?"

Still crying, Eric nodded.

Bessie went on, "Boy, you've caused enough heartache. My granddaughter died using that mess you've been selling. Now get outta here."

We left Eric in the alley.

The next afternoon, Miss Bessie and I shared a boilermaker together. It was her and Sadie's favorite beverage. "Miss Bessie, where did you learn to shoot like that?"

"Roger, when we first moved to this community, our husbands worked long hours. There was a little Klan activity in the area, too. So your grandpa and my husband would take us to a firing range on Sunday after church. Sadie and I became pretty good."

"Yes, you did. Thank you."

"Sugar, don't thank me. I only did what Sadie would have done."

Miss Bessie was full of surprises; I guess I needed to pay more attention.

I left my office an hour early. From the office, I stopped at the Reading Terminal to pick up something to prepare for supper. I also purchased 10 pounds of boneless rib eye and other materials necessary to prepare my contribution for Thanksgiving.

For supper, I prepared lemon roasted chicken, broccoli and garlic mashed potatoes. I also pulled together a garden salad. On the walk home I stopped to pick up a bottle of South African white wine. When Lenora entered the house she was greeted by the aroma of roast chicken and a cold glass of white wine.

"That's more like it." Lenora said.

We kissed and then sat down to eat.

During supper I asked Lenora about her day. Once she had chronicled her day I suggested, "Let's take a ride up to Mount Airy on Saturday and see if we can find Juanita and Mariela."

"Okay, that sounds like a plan."

"By the way, what time is your sister arriving?

"I believe her flight gets in early tomorrow. We can pick her up at her hotel and then fetch Miss Bessie."

CHAPTER SEVEN

On Thursday, Lenora, Liz and I arrived at Miss Bessie's home at three o'clock on the dot. I helped her into the car. Lenora carried the collard greens. When Miss Bessie sat in the car, she was greeted by Liz and Eva Cassidy singing, *God Bless the Child.* Miss Bessie said, "That's one of my favorite songs."

Liz commented, "I like that, too."

Miss Bessie said nothing else until we all arrived at Brandi's. Thom, his partner, Richard, along with JT, Third and Brandi's husband were watching the football game. The Lions made a game of it for awhile but as usual they lost. Thanksgiving is always fun. This year was special because Lenora's sister, Liz was joining us. It is always nice to have a new face in the crowd.

At four-thirty we all gathered around the table, adults and children. Miss Bessie agreed to bless the food. Everyone ate too much. Around eight there was a litany of thank you's and goodbyes. I congratulated Brandi on her successful meal. "Thanks, Uncle." We gathered Liz and Miss Bessie and proceeded to 33rd Street. I parked the car. Then Lenora and I walked Miss Bessie home. As we were saying good night, I asked, "So were you a popular singer years ago?"

"Roger it's late. Can we talk about this some other time? Thank you all for a lovely day."

With that she closed her door. We waited until she locked the door then walked up the street to my house. Since it was the weekend, Lenora and I would stay on 33rd Street. Lenora drove Liz to her hotel. They agreed to meet for a Black Friday shopping safari the following day. Lenora believed it was their civic duty to end the nation's recession all by themselves. We agreed to use Saturday to search Mount Airy for Mariela and Juanita.

CHAPTER EIGHT

Lenora was up at five on Friday morning. By six she was out the door and on her way into town to meet Liz. As she was leaving, "Roger, be sure to keep your cell phone on today." I was still half asleep.

"Ah, okay. Why?"

"I may not be able to carry everything that we buy today on SEPTA. So I want you on standby if we need a lift."

"Now I get it. Your bargain hunting may require me to serve as your beast of burden."

"Exactly! I'll talk with you later." She gave me a kiss and was off and running.

I finally got out of bed around eight. Before showering I went through my exercise routine. I had begun to follow it while on death row. For reasons that escaped me back then, I wanted to be physically fit when the State of Pennsylvania gave me a lethal injection. I guess being on death row made me crazy in some odd way. After my hour-long work out, I showered and had breakfast.

Malik came by at about eleven. He looked good. He was still filling out – growing into manhood. It was always amazing to watch young people mature.

I marveled every time I saw Brandi's children and Malik after not seeing them for a few weeks. "Roger, are you okay? You've got a funny look on your face."

I was unaware that I had been staring.

"Malik, sorry! I'm fine. It's good to see you. Please come in."

"Do you have stuff lined up for me at the office?"

"You bet your ass I do. How's school?"

"Things are cool. I really like the pre-law courses. My work with the Defender's Association has been a big help at times."

"Is Tamika still pre-med?" Tamika, a West Philly gal, had been Malik's girlfriend for a few years.

"Oh yeah! She's working her butt off. We've got a contest going to see who can graduate with the highest GPA."

"Is that good for your relationship?"

"It's fine! If anything we're closer now. I'm going to West Philly in about an hour to meet her."

"How's your mother doing? Did you all have a nice Thanksgiving?"

"We sure did. Can I be honest with you?"

I nodded.

"I never thought that I'd miss my little brother and sister, but I do. They're growing up so fast."

With that I smiled.

"Roger you've got that look again. Are you sure you're not coming down with something?"

"I'm fine. It's just good to see you. As for the office, we've got a few interesting things to keep you occupied."

"Well I'm ready. Roger, do you ever miss being able to practice law?"

"Sure I do! I loved it and at times I was very good. However my work as an investigator/paralegal is almost as satisfying. When I took the oath to become an attorney, I promised to obey and follow the letter and the spirit of the law. When I killed Larry, I broke my sacred oath. So I can live with the consequences of my actions. Besides, I'm still helping people and that was the reason I went to law school in the first place."

"I hear what you're saying. But it seems like you paid your debt and should be given a second chance."

"I am getting a second chance. I'm getting that through you, Angela, Thom, and all of our clients."

Malik paused to think about what I had just said. "You know I see your point. But it still just doesn't seem fair."

“That’s nice of you to say but I’m not completely on the sidelines. Look, we’ve helped Harrison, Jayson and hundreds of others. I’m good with that.”

“Well I just stopped by to let you know I’m back and ready to go.”

“Great! Malik, do you know much about the Mount Airy section of Philly?”

“No sir. I read somewhere that during the late sixties and early seventies it was believed to be the first positive example of an integrated neighborhood in America. But I’ve only been there a few times. Our family is small and we’re all still in North Philly.”

“Well you know more than I do. So thanks.”

“Anytime – I’m heading out to West Philly. Please tell Lenora that I said hi.”

“I will and we’ll meet bright and early in the office on Monday.”

Around two-thirty Lenora and Liz sent out an SOS so I jumped into my car to rescue my damsels in distress. When I reached them, they looked tired but content. First I dropped Liz off at her hotel. Liz lives in Boston and flew down for the Thanksgiving and Black Friday festivities. We agreed to swing by again around seven. Our plan was to have supper at a new Center City restaurant called, “Tweed.”

Liz has been impressed by the various wall murals she’d seen while riding around Philly. She arranged a tour by Mural Arts to see more of them prior to getting together for supper.

Lenora and I arrived back on 33rd Street by three-thirty. I was muttering to myself as I helped Lenora carry her bounty from the safari into the house. She jokingly said, “Roger you are my hero. I don’t know what little old me would do without my big strong husband to help at times like this.” I hissed at her and kept on moving.

CHAPTER NINE

Saturday morning, we got on the road for Mount Airy by ten thirty. Lenora had run the address we'd been given by Bobalu through MapQuest. I drove south, down 33rd Street along Fairmount Park. At Girard Avenue near the Philadelphia Zoo, we picked up Interstate 76 and drove north towards Valley Forge. Mount Airy is just north of Germantown. Lenora read the directions. We took Washington Lane to West Mount Airy Road. When we found our destination, I parked. We both got out of the car and walked towards the house number we'd been given. I had not been to Mount Airy when growing up in Philly. It appeared to be a nice community. Pretty houses, clean streets and the neighborhood seemed to have a diverse population. I knocked on the door of the house at 1973. A teenage girl answered the door. She looked to be about fourteen. She was a pretty young lady. Her smile was beautiful and her skin mocha in color. She did look like the little girl in Bobalu's picture but being unsure, I asked, "Are you Mariela?"

"No and who wants to know?" She said this with an attitude. I nevertheless continued.

"I'm sorry young lady if I offended you. My wife and I are looking for Mariela and her mother Juanita."

The young woman relaxed.

"They moved about a year ago. Miss Juanita got a job at St. Joseph's College. Shortly after that they bought a house on Allen's Lane."

"Do you have or know anyone who may have their address?"

She hesitated, "Are they in trouble?"

"No, no! This is good news."

She appeared suspicious and hollered.

"Hey, Ma! There's some people asking about Juanita and Mariela?"

An older, thinner but just as attractive, woman came to the front door.

"My name is Roger Work and this is my wife Lenora. We've been asked to deliver something to Juanita and Mariela. We have a sizable sum for them. This is not a trick. If you can help, we and they would be appreciative."

"Mister, I don't know you or your wife, do you have some identification?"

I produced my driver's license and Defender's Association business card.

She looked at each carefully.

With a sassy tone, "Is Juanita in some kind of trouble? You handed me this Defender's card. Is this a trick?"

"No ma'am this is not a trick. To my knowledge she is not in trouble. I'm sorry if my business card alarmed you. I was only trying to make sure that you knew who I was."

"They rented here a few years ago. Then Juanita got that good job with the college and she could afford to do better."

I looked around. This area looked pretty nice to me. But I was trying to win this woman's trust. I kept my observations to myself.

"Please, Miss, please help us. I can understand your concern but this really is good news."

"I'll call Juanita. This card has your phone number right?"

"Yes!"

"If she wants to see you, then she can give you her address."

"Thanks! That's fair enough."

With that, we said goodbye and continued to drive around the area. We both liked what we saw. Between our two houses we could afford something out this way.

Later in the afternoon, we stopped in the Sedgwick Theater area. I'd heard some good things about the setting and there was reportedly good dining in addition to what was going on at the theater.

We hung around for awhile before heading back to North Philly. Lenora and I promised to take Liz to the airport early Saturday evening.

I was happy to have Liz join us for the holiday. Liz and Lenora had been very close at one point. When Lenora's first husband died, she withdrew from everyone including family. Lenora initiated the reconciliation after I asked her to marry me. For Lenora this had been a special Thanksgiving. I was very happy for her and Liz. As they say, you can choose your friends but not your family. The farewell at the airport was tearful in a happy way. I looked forward to seeing Liz again.

As we said our goodbyes, I promised Liz and Lenora that we'd visit Boston this summer. While I didn't enjoy Boston during my college years, Lenora was a Bostonian. She hadn't been back home in years. I knew that she yearned to see other members of her family. So we'd fly or drive up sometime over the summer. I had a few classmates who remained in the area and we stayed in touch over the years. I was looking forward to seeing some of them, too.

CHAPTER TEN

Things had been hectic since our return from Florida. Lenora and I were bordering on exhaustion. I guess we needed a vacation from our vacation. We stayed in bed and watched the Sunday morning news shows. Both of us hadn't really had the opportunity to get caught up on national events. In general, we took things easy on Sunday – brunch and watching the Eagles on the tube. The usual couch potato Sunday activities.

As evening approached, I gathered a few things to take with us to Lenora's for the start of another work week. During the ride over, she asked, "Are you excited about having Malik back in the fold?"

"Yes, I enjoy having him at work. He's leaning toward a career as a lawyer. I'm flattered to have been a positive influence on him. But in truth, I've gained more out of our friendship than he. He's smart and doesn't mind working hard. But his greatest asset is he's curious about everything. A good lawyer should be willing to explore all avenues to provide the client with zealous representation."

Once home, Lenora began doing her nesting thing. I smartly got out of her way. We retired for the evening after the 11 o'clock news.

CHAPTER ELEVEN

Malik and Angela were chatting when I arrived in the office on Monday morning. There was a good vibe between the two young people. Angela interrupted her conversation with Malik to let me know that Thom already had a job for Malik. "Fine! Malik once you've met with Thom we can get together and review your other work assignments."

Thom and Malik got together around 9:15. Thom began, "Malik, I need you to review the state's guidelines on securing a Governor's Pardon. We've got an old client that I think may now be eligible under the law. If I'm right, this will be huge for him."

Malik responded, "Okay, Thom, how quickly do you want this information?"

"There's no emergency but the sooner the better. It's nice to have you back, young man."

"I really appreciate how you and others have gone out of your way to make me feel like part of the family here."

"It's been our pleasure. Now get to work."

Malik walked down the hall towards Roger's office.

"Roger, so what would you like me to do?"

I handed him the forensic magazine I'd been reading.

"Malik, do you know the definition of a lawyer?"

"No!"

"It's someone who didn't like math or science."

"Very funny, Roger."

"I'm serious. We're going to have to reduce all of this scientific mumbo jumbo to something that Thom can understand and use. Take a look at this article outlining the problems relating to ballistic and fingerprint analysis. I'd like you to read it carefully. There are some names of experts mentioned in the article. Make a list of their names and then Google them. We may need to talk with them. Before going on our honeymoon to Key

West, a bank robbery case came into our office and it appears to have some interesting wrinkles."

"Sure, Roger. It's great to be back."

"It's good to have you around, Malik."

"Is it okay if I do a little legal research for Thom first?"

"Of course, he's our boss so get going and you can look at these materials later."

The phone rang. Angela buzzed, "There's a Juanita Ramirez on line two for you."

"Thanks!"

I hit the button on my phone marked two.

"Roger Work here."

"Mr. Work this is Juanita Ramirez, are you one of the people working on my daughter's appeal?"

I was initially caught off guard. I had forgotten about the trip to Mount Airy over the weekend.

"Ms. Ramirez, thank you for returning my call. I know nothing about an appeal."

Clearly disappointed Juanita asked, "Then why were you looking for me?"

"I have twenty thousand dollars for you and your daughter. A few weeks ago, I met your husband OJ, and he gave me a check for you and Mariela."

"Wait, let me get this straight; you were looking for me because of my ex?"

"Yes ma'am."

Juanita was now frosty.

"You can send the check to my office. What I need now is help in figuring out how to get Mariela out of Children's Community Center in upper Bucks County."

"I'll be glad to mail you the check. Can you share with me what's going on with Mariela? I'm surprised, given what her father told me."

“What the heck would he know about us? We haven’t seen him in years. I called you because your card indicated that you worked for the Defender’s Association and my daughter needs help. I assumed that Attorney Swift had contacted you.”

“She did not but I would like to help. Can you tell me what’s going on?”

“My daughter is in prison for shoplifting – that she didn’t do. And even if she had this was a first offense.”

“Ma’am that’s highly unusual. What happened?”

“Juvenile Court Judge Jessie O’Brien sentenced her to three months at the Triple C ten days ago. I’ve been trying to get her out ever since.”

“Ms. Ramirez please forgive my ignorance but what is the Triple C?”

“Children’s Community Center, it’s a prison for children.”

“What did you say your daughter’s lawyer’s name was?”

“Darlene Swift.”

“Is it okay if I contact her?”

“Yes, if you can help please do.”

“I will try. I’m very sorry to learn that Mariela is in trouble. I hoped that our meeting would be a happy moment for everyone. In addition to providing me with Ms. Swift’s number can you e-mail or fax me permission to talk with her?”

“Mr. Work I’ll do anything if you can help my daughter.”

“Okay! Our fax number is on the card. Please give me a number where I can reach you and I’ll get on this right away.”

“Thank you so much.”

Roger hung up the phone and waited for the fax. Talking to himself, “Sweet Lord, are we now locking up children for shoplifting?”

CHAPTER TWELVE

"I opened the Lawyer's Diary on my desk and looked up the phone number for Attorney Darlene Swift. I placed a call but got her voicemail. "Hello this is Roger Work. I'd like to talk with you about a client named Mariela Ramirez-James. I may be able to help. You can reach me at the Philadelphia Defender's Association." It was nearly lunchtime so I called Thom's partner Richard, a juvenile court judge.

"Judge's lobby, may I help you?"

"I'd like to speak with Judge Richard Allen please."

"Who's calling?"

"Please tell him it's Roger Work."

"One minute."

"Roger, what a pleasant surprise. Thom and I really enjoyed Thanksgiving."

"We love having you guys around. We're all family."

"That's very kind of you to say."

"It's true!"

"So what's going on?"

"Richard what is Triple C?"

"It's a mess! The city really screwed up when the Mayor and City Council agreed to sign on to a detention facility with Bucks and Delaware Counties. At the time everyone thought this was a way to save money and improve the quality of services for our at-risk children. The Children's Community Correction Program is privately owned and operated. All of us call it Triple C. They have about two hundred juveniles in custody. It's been an unmitigated disaster."

"In what way?"

"First, the city's kids are being held in a place that's more than fifty miles away. So there's limited family contact, unless someone has a car. I've heard that the level of abuse and violence there is off the chart. Lastly, some of my colleagues on the bench seem awfully quick to sentence a child to Triple C."

"Why are they doing that?"

"Truthfully, I don't know, but I've got a bad feeling, Roger. I've never sent a child there. The whole thing makes me uncomfortable."

"Do you know whether any agencies are investigating Triple C?"

"To my knowledge, there are no probes at the moment."

"It sounds like there should be some kind of an investigation."

"You're right. Unfortunately, Roger, your office doesn't handle juvenile cases so the agency in the best position to raise questions is not a player."

"I've been asked by a friend to check on his daughter. Ten days ago she was sent there. It was a first offense – shoplifting."

"Are you sure?"

"No, but I'm going to look into it."

"Tread lightly my friend. There are some powerful people associated with the program. I've got a bad feeling about the whole deal – if you come across anything concrete let me know. I will bring the Feds into this in a heartbeat."

"That does sound bad. It sounds like you don't trust the local authorities. I don't know whether to laugh or cry, but I'll keep your advice in mind."

"Okay, Roger. By the way, please make sure Thom eats the lunch I made for him. He's got to stop eating those damn cheese steaks before they kill him."

"I'll do what I can, but you know Thom."

"Yes, I do. Take care, Roger."

I realized that my hunger alarm was sounding. It was time to get lunch. I decided to walk over to the Record Museum at Tenth and Chestnut, at least that was my recollection. On the way I could stop and get a bite to eat. After grabbing a sandwich, I continued my stroll down Chestnut Street. When I arrived at Tenth and Chestnut I was disappointed. The Record

Museum was no longer there. A sign informed folks that the Record Museum had gone digital. The name of a website appeared on the notice.

I still had a chance to find Miss Bessie's recording of "*Someone to Watch Over Me*" but I'd have to go online to do it.

In my youth, I used to enjoy browsing through the museum's vinyl record collection. The decorative jackets – called "lines" often held treasures waiting to be discovered.

When Big Roger, my dad, was stationed in Seattle at the end of World War II, he played trumpet and drums at a night spot called the Washington Union Social Club, near Jackson Square. Back then, Jackson Square was a place where a number of big-name jazz musicians would perform after completing their concerts for the wealthy folks at Seattle's version of Carnegie Hall. Segregation was not as big of a problem in Seattle as other cities in the lower forty eight states. Nevertheless, performers like Count Basie and Duke Ellington could be found relaxing and jamming at the Washington Union Social Club. The clientele was integrated and everyone felt comfortable letting their hair down. Big Roger used to tell stories about playing sometimes with Jack McVey's Big Band. Few people on the East Coast had ever heard of Jack McVey. During one of my infrequent visits to Philadelphia after completing college and law school, I stopped by the Record Museum. Much to my delight, I found a couple of albums recorded by McVey and purchased them. Several weeks later I gave them to Big Roger as a birthday present. I could never remember seeing dad as happy as he was on that particular day.

I hoped to do the same for Miss Bessie. But I'd have to wait a little longer. The memory of Big Roger stayed with me the rest of the day. Once I returned to the office, I went online to place an order for Miss Bessie's record. At the same time, I ordered recordings by Sarah Vaughn and Gloria Lynne. When growing up after attending church on Sunday, Big Roger would play the albums of these two women. He was always happy listening to the tunes. Sometimes he'd sing along. Occasionally, Big Roger would tell us about his days in Seattle. My sister, Maria and I would frequently join him in singing the last verse of Miss Lynne's song, "*The Folks Who Lived On The Hill.*"

We'd all laugh. Sundays were special in our family. Placing the order reminded me that I had not spoken with my sister in months. She lives in Los Angeles. Things have been strained between us since I killed Larry. She has never really forgiven me. Larry was a pain and Maria would be the first to agree. His antics had frightened her at times. But she loved him anyway. Larry was Brandi's dad. My actions, in addition to ending Larry's miserable life, had also killed Maria's dream of reuniting with him. I needed to call her.

My lunch hour walk had not been without its reward. I merely would have to adjust to having a dream deferred. Besides, Miss Bessie still hadn't acknowledged that she had been a Jazz/R&B singer.

CHAPTER THIRTEEN

Malik knocked on Thom's door shortly before the end of the day.

"Come in."

"Thom, I have the information you requested."

"Okay, Malik, tell me what you've learned."

"Your client would be eligible for a governor's pardon if the conviction is ten or more years old. You can file a petition with the Governor's Office for Pardons."

"Beyond the time requirement what else is a pre-requisite?"

"Well, you or your client would have to document all the good deeds he or she has done since the date of their conviction. How has the person been an asset to the community? It sounds simple, but you'll need to be really convincing. Governor's pardons are rare and almost impossible for a convicted murderer."

"Okay, Malik, can you leave me a copy of the materials you pulled together?"

"Everything is right here, Thom. If it's okay I'm going home. I'll see you tomorrow."

"Goodnight, Malik and thanks. This will save me a lot of time. Thanks again."

* * *

"Mr. Work, this is attorney Darlene Swift. I'm returning your call."

"Thank you!"

What can I do for you? Your message indicated that you wanted to help with Mariela's case."

"Yes, that's right. I spoke with her mother. Ms. Ramirez has given me permission to talk with you."

"She let me know that you called. So how can you help Mariela?"

"Ms. Swift, I don't know that I can but I'd like to try."

"Alright! So?"

"It seems odd to me for a first-time offender to get time for shoplifting. This would not happen to an adult. I'm trying to understand what happened."

"Honestly, I don't know. Judge O'Brien is known for being tough but I never expected this. But since the three counties contracted with Children's Community Center for services, we're seeing more of these perversions happen."

"My understanding is that Triple C is run by a for-profit corporation."

"That's correct, Mr. Work."

"Why did that happen?"

"Delaware, Bucks and Philadelphia Counties are saving millions of dollars a year because they no longer have to fund the infrastructure and overhead for dealing with troubled children."

"Have you researched who serves on Triple C's boards?"

"No! I've been busy with other clients and trying to figure out a way to get Mariela out of lock up." She said defensively.

"Would you mind if I tried to learn the identities of the board members and their relationship with any of the City's elected officials?"

"I can't stop you – though it's hard to see how this will help. But thank you anyway."

"I'll get back to you if I learn anything you might find helpful. I've never met Mariela but this situation is disgraceful."

"I agree with you on that point. I feel bad about what happened. But I'm only one lawyer with very limited resources."

"I understand. But you're not in this by yourself anymore."

"Thank you, Mr. Work. I look forward to hearing from you."

With that Ms. Swift hung up the phone. I sat staring into space. Wondering where to start? I noticed the time. It was after six o'clock. I called Lenora and told her I'd be home within the hour.

After supper, I asked Lenora what she thought we ought to do.

"Have you considered contacting Irene?"

“Why?”

“Roger, she is the Director of the Juvenile Law Project.”

“I forgot.”

“Duh!”

CHAPTER FOURTEEN

Irene and I met during our first year at Delaware State Law School. Because our last names began with an "R" and "W" we were in the same classes for the first two years of school. Irene and I learned that our views, interests and passions were similar and began dating after our second year of school. Irene was the most attractive woman in my class. We didn't give a second thought to being a bi-racial couple. Fiery Irene was the apple of my eye. Irene wanted to work with disenfranchised communities – so legal services work was a natural attraction for her. I also cared about those living on the margins of society. However, I opted to work within the system and went to work for a white-shoe law firm. My clients were wealthy, white-collar criminals. I was often successful representing one of these titans of industry or one of their arrogant and dumb offspring who had gotten into trouble. Many were so grateful that I urged them to support one of Irene's non-profit, tax exempt agencies or causes. Rich people love tax shelters. While Irene was doing God's work, his many children in need could not afford to pay Irene or her colleagues.

Ours was a Ying and Yang relationship at its best. We married after law school. At our wedding we were surrounded by classmates, family and friends. We did well financially. Normally an attorney in legal services doesn't make big bucks. But with me working in downtown Baltimore where the big dogs ran, we had the resources to pay off our law school debt and buy a home. We were happy together. In 1998, when I was arrested, charged and convicted of murder, Irene stood by my side. Although petite and youthful with red curly hair, she's as tough as nails. She often visited me while I was awaiting execution. As time passed I could see the toll all of this was taking on her and begged her to divorce me. Eventually, we agreed that would be best for both of us. We could never be lovers again, but would always be friends.

One of the first phone calls I made upon my unexpected release from prison was to Irene. By then, Irene had a new partner and was the Executive Director of Philadelphia's Juvenile Law Advocacy Project. JLA's primary mission was to work for the adoption of public policies and laws designed to protect juveniles both in and outside the Juvenile Justice System. There are times when attorneys of JLA represent children in delinquency proceedings where potentially ground breaking decisions are possible. JLA is like the NAACP's Legal Defense fund. Instead of focusing on race they protect the rights of children. Often they take on cases and causes that private attorneys don't have the time or expertise to handle properly.

As soon as I arrived at my office, I picked up the phone and dialed Irene's office.

"Good morning JLA may I help you?"

"Irene! Why are you answering your own phone? You're the Director?"

"Roger, sweetie my hands work just fine. I don't need any help. What's going on?"

"Girl, it's good to hear your voice."

"Okay, now I know I'm in trouble. Roger, talk to me. I still love you, too. Let's dispense with the bull. Talk to me."

"What is Triple C?"

"Roger, what are you cooking up? The last time I checked your office only represented adults. Are you and Thom looking to lose a case because of an ineffective assistance of counsel?"

"Of course not! Why would you say that?"

"You and Thom probably know less about juvenile law than my clients."

"Ouch! I forgot how sarcastic you can be."

"Sorry! Did I hurt your feelings?"

"A little."

At that point we both laughed. We'd been playing telephone games for years.

"A friend of mine has a daughter who was sentenced to three months detention at Triple C for shoplifting. It was her first offense."

"Let me guess. Was it Judge O'Brien?"

"How could you possibly know? There are over twenty juvenile court judges in Philadelphia alone?"

"I've been monitoring his cases for a few years. He's the worst offender when it comes to judicial excess."

"How?"

"We've done a review of cases handled by O'Brien for the last three years. He's consistently handing out the harshest juvenile dispositions in the city. But he's not alone. Judges Frank Mara and John Ring are right behind him. If this small group of jurists alone stopped working tomorrow, I'd wonder if Triple C would go out of business."

"Really?"

"I admit, I might be exaggerating a little because there are a few judges in Delaware and Bucks County who are just as bad. But it does make me wonder."

"Why hasn't your office done something?"

"We're working on it. But you have to remember we're largely a policy organization. We don't have a large enough sampling or a clean enough case to pursue it officially. I'm just telling you what I feel in my gut."

"Does your office have anyone actively investigating these judges?"

"No – not at the moment. Wait a minute! Are you thinking about digging deeper into this?"

"Yes, I am. I can't believe the state is locking up children for shoplifting. That's outrageous."

"I agree. So what do I have to say to convince you to take up the cause, my love?"

"Not much. I was going to take some vacation time over the holidays, so I'll look under a few rocks and see what I can find. I spoke with Judge Richard Allen and he has a bad feeling about this, too."

"Are Richard and Thom still together?"

"Yes! They appear to be as happy as any married couple I know."

“Speaking of marriage how’s Lenora?”

“She’s doing well. It was Lenora who prompted me to call you.”

“She’s a smart woman. Please give her my regards.”

“I will – How’s your love life?”

“Funny you should ask. Maxwell and I have decided we’re getting married this Spring. I hope you can be there to walk me down the aisle and give me away?”

“Oh, Irene, I’d be honored. Are you sure? Absolutely! I’ll be there.”

“Thank you, Roger – I’ll always love you.”

“Me too.”

“Okay enough with the mushy stuff. I’ll be in touch with the details. In the meantime, if you need help with your investigation don’t hesitate to call.”

“I won’t – we’ll talk later and congratulations!”

I hung up the phone, my eyes a bit misty.

CHAPTER FIFTEEN

Moments later, Thom entered my office.

"Richard told me about some juvenile thing. What's going on?"

"While Lenora and I were on our honeymoon we met a guy from Philly who asked us to do a favor for him. At the time it seemed like a good idea – a Mitzvah – you know, a good deed from the heart."

"Roger, when did you start speaking Yiddish?"

"After all the years I've been around you and Irene, I've learned a few things."

"So what are you doing?"

"I was trying to find a little girl and her mother. I have a $20,000 check for them."

"Wow."

"Yeah, wow."

"So?"

"I found the mother but the daughter is in juvenile lockup for shoplifting. And to make things worse this is her first offense of any kind."

"Please tell me you're kidding?"

"No sir! That's the truth."

"I don't follow juvenile case law very closely, but did I miss something?"

"We all did, apparently. This has been going on for some time. The city, along with Delaware and Bucks Counties, entered into a contract for five million a year with a private company called Children's Community Center – Triple C – to detain and provide food, shelter and other necessities to the juveniles sentenced to their custody. Like all privatization schemes, it was supposed to save taxpayers millions of dollars. I don't know if any money has, in fact, been saved. I do know that a bunch of kids are getting a raw deal."

"This is unbelievable. What are you going to do?"

"With your permission, I'd like to look into this in my spare time. It'll require me to have access to some of our office resources. Is that okay?"

"Of course, Roger – although we don't represent juveniles, too often things like Triple C help to drive clients our way. Young offenders who are mistreated often grow into adult offenders. Who knows, maybe you'll end up reducing our caseload. Let me know what you need."

"Thanks, Thom."

"Don't thank me. Last night Richard swore he'd only serve me salads at night if I didn't help. This is purely self-defense."

"By the way, on the bank robbery case, I think we should file a *Daubert* Motion."

"Why? There's ballistic and fingerprint evidence."

"That's exactly why. Malik and I have reviewed several scientific journals and magazines. There appears to be a consensus emerging that all of the so-called science underlying fingerprint and ballistic analysis is not grounded in hard science. No one can find anything to suggest that their stuff is based on true sciences like biology, chemistry or physics. Apparently, it is all 'junk-science'."

"Holy crap! Are you saying that this evidence is unreliable and therefore inadmissible?"

"Yeah! Thom, you're probably representing an innocent man unless there's something else to link him to the bank robbery. Remember there are no photos and the perp was wearing that outrageous Philly Phanatic costume. Our client was arrested days after the bank robbery at his home. He had a gun, that was licensed but there was no cash or costume found. Best of all, he had an alibi."

"You're saying another dude did it?"

"Perhaps. What I'm saying for sure is the government has a case that they can't prove beyond a reasonable doubt and that's all we need. There's so much reasonable doubt here Malik could handle the case."

"That's a nice thought on which to end a day. I'll see you later. Good luck with that juvie thing."

"Good night, Thom."

CHAPTER SIXTEEN

I spent much of the following day pulling together everything I had on the bank robbery case for Thom. Using several three ring binders I assembled everything I had on the forensic piece, the alibi witness and drafts of motions designed to have the case dismissed. Around three I asked Malik to join me.

"Do you know anything about the juvenile courts here?"

"Not much – I used to hear things about a couple of judges that people felt were shady. But that's it."

"Tell me why they were shady?"

"Well people wondered if they were getting money under the table for sending juvenile delinquents to Triple C. I never asked why. What's goin on?"

I told Malik about OJ, Juanita, Mariela and Judge O'Brien. As I wrapped up my story an idea came to me.

"Have we ever had you look at articles of incorporation and Board of Trustee materials kept at the Secretary of State's Office?"

"Not that I can recall."

"I didn't think so. Tomorrow I want you spend as much time as you can researching who owns and controls Triple C."

"Sure just point me in the right direction and I'll get started first thing in the morning."

"Okay!"

"You've been here almost two weeks and I haven't taken you to lunch or dinner. Do you have plans tonight?"

"No."

"Let's grab something to eat. Lenora's got a board meeting at the Zoo, so I'm unattached for the evening. Besides it's almost Christmas and we should break bread together before you have to go back to school."

"Great let's go. Ms. Lenora doesn't seem like a board joining person."

"She's not but after her husband's death years ago, Lenora started visiting the Zoo once a week and it became one of her favorite causes. Eventually, someone from the Zoological Society invited her to join their board and she did. So, back to dinner, is there any place in particular that you'd like to try?"

"No, you pick it – and I'll eat it."

"Good, let's get out of here."

We ended up dining at Ms. Tootie's on South Street about a five minute walk from the office. Ms. Tooties' is an upscale soul food restaurant. I'd been craving fried chicken just like Grandma Sadie used to make and Ms. Tootie's fried chicken was the next best thing.

After dinner, I made sure Malik got home safely and then I turned in myself. Now that Thom's project was under control, immediately after the holidays I could sink my teeth into Mariela's problem. First I'd get her out of the custody of Triple C and then I'd investigate if something shady was going on between Triple C and some of the local judges. Tomorrow was Friday. I was looking forward to the weekend.

* * *

We spent Christmas Eve and most of Christmas Day on 33rd Street. I prepared a meal fit for a queen on Christmas Eve. Prior to our dinner we decorated our first Christmas tree together. Lenora brought some of her favorite ornaments from her house. We used a few of Grandma Sadie's. As a final touch we used some of our newly acquired Key West decorations. We had a wonderful first Christmas. Christmas Day we spent time with Brandi and her family.

New Year's Eve we stayed at Lenora's. The fireplace was cozy. We had a champagne toast at midnight and watched the city's fireworks show from the rear window of the bedroom.

CHAPTER SEVENTEEN

Philly's January thaw came early. As Lenora and I were leaving our house on 33rd Street, we ran into Miss Bessie.

"Good morning, Miss Bessie and Happy New Year."

"Back at you, son."

"Why are you up so early this morning?"

"Children, I couldn't resist taking a little walk. It's such a nice morning we might not have another day like this for weeks. Isn't the park so pretty today?"

"Yes it is, ma'am." Chimed in Lenora.

"Is everything okay otherwise?"

"It sure is – you all better get to work before you lose your jobs. Times are hard. People need to be careful. It's not easy finding a good job after you reach a certain age ya know."

I said, "As always, you're right. It's a pleasure to see you this morning. You have a nice day."

We ran to catch the bus.

* * *

Malik would have to return to college in a few days. He wanted to take care of his assignment for me before going back to Lincoln University. With the help of his girlfriend Tamika he was able to locate Pennsylvania's Secretary of State's Office. The people at the office were friendly and helpful. There was one awkward moment though. A fellow who worked in the office wanted to know why he was interested in the incorporation documents pertaining to Children's Community Center.

"Sir, I'm working for Mr. Work at the Defender's Association."

Tamika held up her hand – "Malik wait! These are public records you don't have to tell this man what you're doing."

"That smart mouth young lady friend of yours is right. You don't have to tell me anything. I was just curious."

The man then turned and walked back to what appeared to be his office.

When he was gone, Tamika said, "You told me that this information might help Roger get a little girl out of Triple C. I'm not sure that you should be telling strangers what you're doing. You never know about people."

"You're right. Roger would have a fit if he knew that I was running my mouth. What was I thinking?"

"I don't know but I wanted to stop you before you went too far."

"Thanks!"

Malik and Tamika left the office of the Secretary of State. Malik had promised to drive her to Willow Grove so she could see her cousin who was also home on college break.

* * *

"Judge O'Brien, this is Rudy Shea from the Secretary of State's Office."

"What do you want?"

"Well, sir, I thought you might want to know a young black man was here earlier and he wanted information on Children's Community Center."

"Did he say why?"

"No sir, when I asked, his lady friend told him to keep his mouth shut."

"Rudy, did the fella happen to mention who he was working for?"

"Sort of, he mentioned a Mr. Work who works for the Defender's Association. This isn't like those other times when we had reporters snooping around."

"Was there anything else?"

I just thought that you might want to know."

"Thank you, Rudy. Do you like hockey?"

"Yes your honor."

"Good, I'll have someone deliver a pair of tickets for the Flyers-Bruins game next week."

"Your honor, that's not necessary."

"I know it isn't, but you went out of your way, so this is just a little thank you."

"Thank you, sir."

As soon as he got off the phone with Rudy, Judge O'Brien called Judge Frank Mara, another Philadelphia Juvenile Judge.

"Frank, we may have a problem, someone was looking into the Children's Community Center over at the Secretary of State's Office. It wasn't a reporter like before. The kid was from the Defender's Association."

"Jessie, why would the Defender's Association be interested in Triple C? They don't handle juvenile cases."

"I don't know but I don't like it."

"What are we gonna do?"

"I'll look into it. Maybe we can stop this before it even gets started."

"That would be a good idea. Do you want me to call John?"

"Not yet, let's not jump the gun."

"Okay! Keep in touch."

CHAPTER EIGHTEEN

Malik arrived at the office around mid-afternoon. He reported to me what he'd learned about the corporate identity of Children's Community Center. I scanned the list of names on the board of trustees and some of them looked vaguely familiar.

Turning to Malik, I asked "Did you have any trouble getting this information?"

"Not really. But a guy, who worked at the Secretary of State's Office, did ask me who I was working for? I was in the process of answering his question when Tamika stopped me. She reminded me that these were public records and I didn't have to say anything."

"I really like that young lady. She was right."

I thanked Malik for his work. "I'll Google some of these names later."

This was Malik's last day in the office until spring break. He was returning to Lincoln University on Sunday to complete his junior year.

"How do you feel about returning to school? Do you have any special plans?"

"Not really. But I'm ready to get back to class. I am planning to take the Law School Admissions Test in February. Last November I took a prep course. I did well."

I was caught off guard. I knew that Malik was leaning toward applying to law school, but taking the test was an indication that he was serious.

"Are you ready for the test?"

"I hope so. That's why I'm taking the test next month. If I don't like my score, I've got two more opportunities to take it before graduation."

"You've really thought this through. I'm impressed."

"Do you have any tips?"

"Yeah, make sure you get plenty of rest before taking the exam. I'm sure you'll do fine."

"I hope so. I want to have choices rather than just settling. There are a few schools that I'd love to be accepted into."

"What do you have in mind?"

"U. Penn, Villanova and Temple are great schools. Any of those would be good. I want to go to a Philly School."

"Why?"

"That way I can work here and still attend classes."

I whistled. "You seem to have it all figured out. Good luck! If there's any way I can help, let me know."

"Roger, you've already done so much. When we met, I was standing on a corner selling drugs. Man, you gave me a chance. I'll never forget that."

"It's been my pleasure. But don't underestimate what you've done. You had to have the courage to step up and take a chance. I know that Blue's murder rocked your world. But you still had to make a choice."

Blue was another drug dealer who had worked on 33rd Street when Malik was dealing. 33rd Street is a main thoroughfare for North Philly. Blue's bullet ridden body had been found in a trash-filled vacant lot around the corner from where he'd been dealing for years. Later we learned that JT's brother, Eric, was responsible. To make things worse, the area police were on Eric's payroll. They hadn't even bothered to investigate the cause of Blue's death.

Continuing our conversation, "Yeah, I remember all of that. But still, you reached out to me."

"So, why do you have that sad dog look? You're only going back to college."

"That's my point, Roger. I'm in college. Three/four years ago that seemed impossible."

I was touched by his sentiment.

"Okay, Malik it's time for you to go. But first, man hugs!"

* * *

Judge O'Brien of Juvenile Court called me towards the end of the day.

“Mr. Work would you please come by my office on Monday? I’d like to discuss a matter with you.”

“Sure, your honor. But our office doesn’t handle juvenile cases.”

“I know, nevertheless, I’d like to see you.”

“Yes sir, I’ll drop by Monday morning before nine.”

“Thank you Mr. Work. I’ll see you then.”

I hung up the phone and stared at it for a moment. How odd that the Judge who started this nightmare for Mariela wanted to see me. I sat there for fifteen minutes trying to figure out what the heck was going on. I decided to wait until Monday to try to unravel the mystery.

Lenora and I had tickets to see Jersey Boys at the Forrest Theater that evening. I grabbed my coat and gloves and rushed out to meet my wife.

CHAPTER NINETEEN

Saturday morning, I walked over to Third's Barbershop. It was time to get a professional shave of my scalp. When I entered the shop business was slow. Only Third and JT were there. I had not seen either since Thanksgiving. We began with our ritual of good-natured ribbing. I told them what I learned about Miss Bessie while in Key West. Third said, "I keep tellin' you guys. You gotta keep your eyes and ears on those old folks. The stories they can tell. If we only knew half of what they've done."

"You're right about that. I've ordered a copy of Miss Bessie's only album. It will be a birthday present for her."

JT who is a musician said, "That's cool." One could always count on JT for understating the obvious. But that's one reason why we've been friends since we were four years old.

I had met Third while in college. When Third finished, he gave me a mirror.

"What do you think?"

"That's good – Thanks."

JT asked, "Roger, are you hosting this year's Super Bowl Party?"

"If I had any sense, given how much you two eat, I'd say no. But sure, it'll be fun. I like the fact that our Eagles are still in the hunt."

Third said, "Okay, so we'll see you then."

"Have either of you guys heard any rumors about juvenile judges doing strange things?"

Third looked at me, "What do you mean by strange?"

"You know people complaining that somebody received a really heavy sentence when the punishment didn't seem to fit the crime."

"Now that you mention it. Mr. Brown, a regular here, was complaining how his great grandson was doing juvie time on a first offense. He claimed that no one was hurt and no property was damaged."

"Did he say anything else?"

"No, not really. To be truthful people are always saying the system screwed them or a relative. So I didn't think much of it."

"Hopefully, Mr. Brown was wrong. While Lenora and I were in Key West we met a guy who grew up in West Philly. He asked us to deliver something to his kid. We tried. Turns out the guy's daughter has been locked up for shoplifting. This was her first arrest and adjudication of delinquency."

JT's eyes nearly popped out of his head. "For real?"

"I'm afraid so."

"Man, that kind of stuff should not be allowed to happen."

"I agree."

"So what are you going to do?" Third asked.

"I don't know. But I've got to do something."

JT said, "Roger you be careful. Don't get yourself into any trouble."

"I hear you. But I've got to fix this. It ain't right."

* * *

I walked from the barbershop up to 34th and Lehigh. The cemetery that was Big Roger's final resting place was quiet. I walked over to my father's headstone.

Big Roger was laughing. *"Son what's your problem?"*

"How come you never told me about Grandma Sadie and Miss Bessie being jazz singers?"

"It wasn't my place to, Junior. Your Grandma and Miss Bessie are entitled to have their secrets."

"I guess you're right, but why hide something like that?"

"People have their reasons and that's good enough for me. It should be for you, too."

"Maybe, but I've always loved music and now I know I've lost the opportunity to talk with Grandma."

"True! But Miss Bessie is around. If you're not too pushy maybe she'll tell you."

"What else is on your mind, son?"

"There's a young women in custody now who shouldn't be there. It's unfair and crazy if you want the truth."

"Roger, my son, I learned a long time ago that everything happens for a reason. Sometimes we're in such a hurry that we don't see the big picture. Are you talking about one child or many?"

"Dad, I don't know."

"Well then, it's time for you to find out. Was it an isolated event or has the system been compromised? In helping one child, one family – you could be looking at the tip of an iceberg."

"I know. That's what scares me. I shudder to think that hundreds of families could have been put through this for no good reason."

"Roger, I taught you never to fear the truth."

"I know. The truth shall set you free."

Big Roger laughed, *"That's my son. It's time for you to get busy."*

I took a few steps back, and paused, *"I miss you, Dad."*

* * *

Lenora and I had a quiet Sunday meal. Lenora asked "Do you want to stay here on 33rd Street tonight or head over to my place in town?"

"Let's go to your place. It'll save both of us a little time in the morning."

CHAPTER TWENTY

Monday morning, I entered the chambers of Judge O'Brien. The judge was bigger than I thought he would be. I couldn't really tell his age because the guy looked washed out. He reminded me of a fella who might have had one too many.

"Mr. Work, thank you for coming to see me."

"It's my pleasure, your honor."

I didn't mean it given what the Judge had done to Mariela but one was always supposed to be respectful to a judge.

"Mr. Work, what's your interest in Children's Community Center?"

"I beg your pardon, your honor." I was caught off guard by his directness.

"Look Work, don't get cute with me. I know that you've been sniffing around one of my cases. What's your beef?"

"Your honor, I'm not sure what you're talking about. But, if you want to know why I'm interested in the Mariela Ramirez-James matter, my beef is her receiving three months confinement at Children's Community Center for a first offense. That seems odd to me."

"So, you say! This is none of your business. If I hear from anyone else about you meddling in mine anymore, I'll see to it that you lose your job. You are a convicted felon and a disbarred attorney. I can't believe that the Defender's hired you to do anything. Have I made myself clear?"

"I guess so, your honor."

"Good! I assume that we will never have to discuss this matter again." O'Brien returned to the papers on his desk. "Well, Mr. Work, thank you for coming by. Have a good day."

As I left the Judge's lobby I was confused and angry. No one likes a bully. Clearly O'Brien was used to getting his way. Only time would tell if that would be the case this time.

* * *

I worked through lunch. Around four, I received a call from Mr. Castaldo – as in Don Giovanni Castaldo. The Don was the head of a South Philadelphia crime family. We had become friends of sorts a year-and-a-half ago.

"Mr. Castaldo, it's good to hear from you. How's your wife and granddaughter? Is there something I can do for you?"

"My family is fine."

"Roger, I'll be direct here. Someone tried to pay one of my people to punch your clock – to put a hit on you. Do you understand what I'm saying?"

"Yes sir, I believe I do. Someone wanted me killed?"

"That's right! They tried to buy a contract. But, no one from my family will touch you. You must be careful, my friend."

"Thank you, Mr. Castaldo."

"Roger, you will always have a warm place in my heart. Take care of yourself and your lovely wife."

I placed the telephone back in the cradle and stared into space. "What the hell is going on?"

After the brief conversation, I was so deep in thought that I didn't notice when Thom came into my office.

"Roger?"

"Huh, what? Oh Thom, I didn't see you."

"Yeah, I noticed. What's going on? You look like you just saw a ghost."

"Maybe I did!"

"Stop the crazy talk. What happened?"

"On Friday I received a call from Juvenile Court Judge Jessie O'Brien."

"What did he want? We don't have any juvie cases."

"I know. The judge asked me – that's putting it kindly – to come by his office today. Since he's a judge I figured no big deal. So this morning, I went there."

"Okay."

"Not okay, that's when the stuff hit the fan. O'Brien's greeting was frosty. But what do I know? Maybe he got up on the wrong side of the bed? The judge starts acting like I'm a fourteen year old in his courtroom. He asked me why I was interested in Children's Community Center. I was surprised. I explained my concern about Mariela. He seemed to know I was interested in Triple C and the case of Mariela Ramirez-James before I said anything. It was a '*Twilight Zone'* moment."

"That is strange."

"Things got worse. The dude threatened me. He knew about my conviction and questioned whether I should be working for the Defender's office. Then, with the subtlety of a sledge hammer, told me if I didn't mind my own business he'd make sure I didn't have a job. After telling me this, he dismissed me like I was a servant."

"Jeez! He can't talk to my staff that way."

"I was stunned by the judge's behavior. But ultimately I figured it didn't matter because we have no cases before him. It's not like he can hurt our clients."

"You're right. Still, I'll start drafting a note to him and copy his Chief Justice. He needs to back off."

"Thanks for the offer, Thom, but there's more."

Sarcastically, "I'm dying to hear this."

"Be careful what you wish for my friend."

Thom stared at me as though I had three heads.

"What else happened?"

"I just received a call from Don Giovanni Castaldo."

"You're kidding?"

"No! A few years ago we worked on that basketball point shaving case."

"Yes, I remember – Jayson Jackson!"

I continued, "Jayson's girlfriend is the Don's granddaughter. I met with the family because of what Jayson confided in me. I believed the Don helped us with Jayson's case. How, I don't know. But I'm sure you remember that Tony Donatelli pled guilty to extortion and a few other things. Of course, it helped that our client was actually innocent. You may recall that the judge forced the government to acknowledge, on the record, Jayson's innocence. She loudly declared Jayson not guilty. The Don was so appreciative that he and his wife sent Lenora and me a wedding gift. Don Giovanni loves his granddaughter and chose to express his appreciation with the gift."

"Where is this going – and do I want to know?"

"The office is fine."

"I can feel a but, Roger."

"You're right! The Don called ten minutes ago to tell me that someone tried to hire one of his people to kill me. Mr. Castaldo told his guy to forget about it."

"Do you have any idea what started all of this?"

"My best guess is, when Malik picked up some documents for me from the Secretary of State's Office, someone contacted Judge O'Brien. Malik mentioned that a staff member stopped him and tried to pry some information from him about his research. Malik was getting copies of all the documents relating to the creation and running of the Children's Community Center. Since it's a corporation, I wanted to see who was on its board."

"What did you find out?"

"I haven't had the opportunity to look at the papers."

"Let's do it now. Is that the pile of documents over in the corner?"

"Yes."

Dividing the pile of papers in half, Thom said, "I'll look through these. You handle the rest."

"Sure – before doing that let me Google the names of the Board of Directors."

"Why?"

"Some of the names looked familiar but I couldn't remember why."

"All right then, you start there."

I booted up my computer and began running names. At first nothing seemed odd. The founder was a rich entrepreneur who supposedly lived in the Delaware Valley. Harry Barr was owner or started up a number of businesses. He'd done well. The second corporate board member's name was a retired Juvenile Court Judge Martin Frost, the chairman of the board. Initially, this didn't faze me either. When I ran the names of the corporation's clerk and treasurer, bells started ringing in my head. Triple C's clerk was retired Juvenile Judge Portia Moore. Their treasurer was William McBride, also a retired juvenile judge. Each judge sat in one of the three counties that signed the contract with Children's Community Center. According to the IRS 1099's tax forms, each incorporator/founder, Moore, McBride and Frost were being paid $250,000 a year for serving on the board. Each of the retired judges were now making almost twice as much as they did when they were on the bench. Another interesting tidbit I noted was that all of the judges at one time or another had supervisory duties in their respective counties.

I quickly drafted a summary of what I'd uncovered and asked Thom to review it. After reading what I had pulled together Thom whistled, "Roger, this can't be right. These guys are dirty."

"I agree but before we jump to any conclusions let me call Irene. She may be able to tell us whether there's any relationship between Judge O'Brien and any of the board members."

"Okay, go for it."

I picked up the phone.

"Irene Roos."

"Irene it's, Roger. Do you have a moment?"

"Sure, Roger, what's up?"

"Let me read you a list of names and tell me if you've heard of them and what you know about them."

I began, "Martin Frost, Portia Moore, and William McBride."

"Is this some kind of game?"

"No, I'am deadly serious."

"Such drama! Okay every name you've given me is a retired Juvenile Court Judge. Two of them, Moore and Frost, worked here in Philly. McBride sat in Bucks or Delaware County, I'm not sure which was O'Brien's mentor. So, how did I do?"

"As always, Irene, you're a wealth of knowledge."

“Skip the flattery. What’s going on?”

“Please keep this to yourself.”

“Okay.”

“Frost, McBride and Moore are all corporate officers of Triple C. Each is making $250,000 serving on the board.”

Irene went silent for a moment. “Did you tell me that O’Brien gave time to a fifteen year old girl on a shoplifting charge, first offense?”

“That’s right.”

“Roger, something is terribly wrong here!”

“Thom and I agree. We’re unsure of what to do.”

“I can’t imagine why!”

“God bless you, Irene. You always were a wise ass.”

“So you’ve said.”

“Well let me share with you this bulletin! I learned a half hour ago that someone wants to kill me.”

“Stop with the jokes, this isn’t funny.”

“I’m not joking. Don Giovanni Castaldo called to tell me that he wouldn’t allow anyone in his family to take the hit.”

“How did you manage to befriend a mobster?”

“At the moment how is not important. I trust the Don. If he says someone wants me offed, I believe him.”

Irene noted the irony, “Only you could stumble into a mess where the bad guys are the good guys and the good guys are bad.”

“Irene, if what you’re saying is how often does an alleged mobster rat out a judge or judges, I agree. It is strange to say the least. Please keep this to yourself. I don’t want the Don involved so if there’s another way to show that something is wrong I’d like a chance to do so.”

“Hey, it’s your call, but help me understand why would you want to protect Don Giovanni Castaldo? Wait, don’t answer that question.”

“Thanks, Irene. I’ll let you know what’s happening before we make any moves.”

“Be careful. Remember you’re supposed to walk me down the aisle in a few months.”

"Don't worry. I'll be there."

Thom asked, "What did Irene tell you?"

"All of them are retired juvenile court judges. Each had supervisory authority while on the bench. O'Brien is a protégée of Frost. Frost was his supervisor."

"Did you read the last paragraph on Barr?"

"No, I just looked to see if the guy existed."

"He did, but he died before Children's Community Center was founded."

"Are you sure? I thought that dead people could only vote in Philly and Chicago. When did they start forming corporations as well?"

"According to this website, the guy was a successful businessman but died several years ago."

"This means that these retired judges formed a dummy corporation and are making all the profits – so they're making more than what's reported on the 1099!"

"It would seem that way."

"What the hell is going on here?"

"I don't know. We should let the District Attorney or the Attorney General knows what we've uncovered."

I thought about what Thom said. "We don't really have anything but a lot of loose ends. There's a threat that can't be used because of my friendship with Don Castaldo. We know that the corporation has a dead incorporator – but it is possible, if you also believe in the Easter Bunny, that prior to Barr's death, he had agreed to participate in this enterprise with the three retired judges. Lastly, we have mean and nasty Judge O'Brien who has a close relationship with retired Judge Frost. Frost happens to be chairman of the board of Triple C. I wish this last item were a crime but if it was we'd have very few judges. As I see it, all we've got is speculation and a bunch of odd events. You and I would love to represent any of these judges. There's nothing tying it all together. Maybe I'll ride up to Triple C on Monday."

"I agree with your conclusion but we can't ignore the threat. Maybe you'll see or learn something while there."

"Maybe we're missing something. This thing has fallen on us like a ton of bricks. Maybe one of us will think of something over the weekend."

"I'll try but you've got to promise that you'll be extra careful."

"I promise. We'll talk about this next week. Your *Daubert* motion is scheduled for Monday, are you ready?"

"Yes, I spoke with all of our experts and I'm confident that the judge will find it hard to disagree. This is an ID case and the circumstantial evidence does not hold up. Yeah, I'm good. Once again your work is outstanding. It's too bad that you can't be readmitted."

"I've come to accept my situation. It seems as though everybody else is having more difficulty with that fact than me."

"Okay buddy! Sorry!"

CHAPTER TWENTY-ONE

Lenora and I got together for dinner with some friends and in a departure from our normal routine we stayed at Lenora's for the weekend.

Early Saturday morning I drove to my place on 33rd Street and picked up my mail. There was a package from the Record Museum. I opened it. There was a record jacket with a photograph of Miss Bessie front and center. Grandma Sadie could be seen standing to the right. The lettering read, "Bessie Smith live at Tally Ho." Also in the box were the Gloria Lynne and Sarah Vaughn CDs I ordered."

I turned to the back of Bessie's jacket where a list of songs recorded included "*Someone to Watch Over Me*." What had originally been recorded as a 78 was now on disc. I was tempted to break the seal on the cover but stopped myself. This was Miss Bessie's birthday present. Her birthday was next Saturday; she would turn eighty-five. Lenora, JT, Third and I had been planning a little celebration for her. I could wait until then to hear the music.

Lenora and I agreed to meet back at her 22nd and Arch Street house mid-afternoon. We each had a honey-do list. I didn't mind this aspect of domestic life. In fact, I had come to enjoy doing our chores together. I had yet to tell Lenora about the phone call from Don Giovanni Castaldo, I was waiting for the right moment. I asked JT, who managed a number of properties on 33rd Street, to keep an eye on my house and be on guard for any strangers hanging around. "Don't worry, brother, I've got your back."

I was comfortable with JT watching things in part because Lenora and I had no plans to stay in North Philly over the weekend.

Around four, Lenora finished up. She turned to me, "What are you attempting to hide? You're not telling me something."

I was surprised and unaware of giving off any strange vibes.

"Miss Bessie's record came today. It was recorded live at Tally Ho."

"Roger, don't play with me. That record has nothing to do with your jumpiness."

"Okay, honey. Sit down. Let's talk. I heard from Don Giovanni Castaldo."

"Roger, you know that I like Mr. Castaldo and his wife, but why would he be calling you? Your office doesn't handle mob cases."

"He didn't call me about a case. The Don wanted to warn me, someone tried to put a contract – a hit – on me."

"What?"

"He said that someone contacted a member of his clan about a hit. Since last year, the Don has been really strict about members of his family freelancing. Fortunately, he told the wiseguy to turn down the job."

"Why would someone want to kill you?"

"I don't know but I'm starting to suspect that it could have something to do with Mariela and my inquiry into her incarceration with Triple C."

"What makes you think that?"

"Yesterday morning I visited with Judge O'Brien. He told me to mind my own business. He also threatened me if I didn't stop asking questions. The judge knew about my prior conviction and said that I shouldn't be working with the Defender's. He implied that could change."

"I don't get it."

"Honey, I don't get it either. Now I wonder if Judge O'Brien has something to hide. If so, it must be really bad."

"I'm worried. If this is related to Mariela then we should contact OJ and let him know that his daughter is in trouble."

"Yeah, I'll call him tomorrow morning. I don't think I'm in immediate danger. Since Don Castaldo has told his people to back off, there's a good chance that no other hit-man in this area would touch the contract. The Don would probably find them long before the police."

"I can see your logic, but I'm still worried."

"Sweets, I'll be okay. My official address is 33rd Street. Anyone looking for me is likely to start there. Just in case, I've asked JT to keep an eye on my place."

"All right, but how about having supper at home tonight rather than going out."

"Sure, baby. If it'll make you feel more comfortable. Besides, I'm tired anyway."

CHAPTER TWENTY-TWO

Sunday morning, I called OJ while Lenora went to the grocery store.

"Bobalu, its Roger Work."

"Hey, Roger, how are you and Lenora doing?"

"We're fine. We found your daughter and your ex."

"Great!"

"Not so great."

"What do you mean?

"Mariela has been locked up in a privately operated facility for children."

"What's the charge?"

"To be truthful OJ, I doubt that she's done anything. But she was sentenced to three months confinement at a place called Children's Community Center for shoplifting."

"Shoplifting?"

"That's right. It was her first offense."

"Damn! Three months for a first offense of shoplifting. Am I missing something?"

"That's why I'm calling. This whole thing stinks and your family needs you. How soon can you get up here?"

"I'll be there in a few days. I don't care about the outstanding warrant. Please let Juanita know."

"I'll call her tomorrow. OJ, by the way, I took care of your non-support warrants."

"Thanks. Where is this Children's Community Center? I want to see my kid."

"It's in Northern Bucks County a place called Hillstown Township."

"Why is she in Bucks County? Aren't Mariela and Juanita still living in Philly?

"Yes they are, but there's a contract between Delaware, Bucks and Philadelphia Counties. The contract shifted care and custody of juveniles to

Children's Community Center. It was supposed to upgrade services while saving the counties money."

"Okay, Roger, thanks. It'll take me a few days but I'll be there as soon as I can. Is this the phone number where I can reach you?"

"I'll be here, OJ."

When Lenora returned from the store I told her about my conversation with OJ. I also let her know of my plan to drive up to Triple C on Monday if Attorney Swift and Mariela's mother gave their consent.

Lenora and I spent the remainder of the weekend together. We were especially affectionate towards each other. I guess knowing you're in someone's crosshairs has a way of bringing a couple closer.

CHAPTER TWENTY-THREE

Lenora insisted that I take a taxi to work on Monday morning. She also called Thom Sunday evening to be sure I had access to an office pool car if I, in fact, drove to Hillstown Township to meet with Mariela.

Once in the office I called Attorney Swift and Ms. Ramirez.
"Mr. Work, I feel bad for Mariela. The system has screwed her. I've filed an appeal but it's not likely to be heard before her release. I'm sure you're familiar with this old trick by judges. You sentence defendants for a period just long enough to make their life miserable but not long enough for an appeal to be of any use. In this state, unless there's something unusual, it takes about ninety days before an appellate court will have a chance to rule on the legality of a matter. For adults, this is a problem because after a prisoner has accumulated enough short sentences, a three strikes situation may arise. If a suspect has three minor felony convictions and they're convicted of a fourth felony then the mandatory life or seventy years in prison sentence kicks in. The client is considered a habitual offender. There's a similar mechanism in our juvenile court system. Even so, many of my clients and their parents don't want to pursue an appeal once the child is back home. In fact, everyone wants to pretend that nothing happened. So the beat goes on – and our criminal justice system continues to grind people down."

"Ms. Swift, I am familiar with the problem, some legal scholars refer to this as a modern version of slavery. At the moment though, I'd just like permission to speak with your client. If you call ahead it would make things easier."

"What do you hope to accomplish?"

"I can't say for sure but Mariela may be in the position now to help me understand a few things. If I'm right, you may be able to get your client out of Triple C in a few days."

"That sounds mysterious, Mr. Work. I don't know what you have in mind but if it will help, I'll call."

"Thank you. I'll get back to you right away if I come across anything that's concrete."

I hung up the phone and looked for Juanita Ramirez's phone number.

"Ms. Ramirez, this is Roger Work. We spoke several weeks ago. I'd like your permission to speak with Mariela. Her attorney has already agreed but I need your permission too."

"Why do you want to talk with my daughter? Have you been up to that horrible place?"

"No, ma'am, I haven't but I'd like to see your daughter anyway."

"That place, the Children's Community Center, is a hellhole and the children are mistreated by the staff and other kids who are staying there. Mariela finally came up with a scheme to keep herself out of the general population. General population consists of large rooms where twelve to fourteen kids sleep. There's supposed to be two guards there at all times, but according to Mariela, that seldom happens. So the bigger/older girls make the new arrivals or the weak girls their servants. She told me that initially someone threatened to mess her up. Fortunately, a girl Mariela knew from our old neighborhood, Francine, recognized her and told this woman, Carrie Kish, to leave Mariela alone. Carrie must have been afraid of Francine because she stopped messin' with Mariela. When Francine was about to be released she explained to my daughter how to arrange to be sent to the medical ward. Francine told her, 'The guards actually do their jobs there, so you'll be safe.'"

I said, "I assume she took Francine's advice."

Juanita, sounding as if she were about to cry, "She certainly did. I go up there every weekend and spend as much time as I can with Mariela. Families can stay for several hours in the morning and afternoon. Besides crying, Mariela sleeps when I'm there. She said to me, 'Ma this is the only time I feel safe.' So, if you want to see my daughter, go ahead. I don't even care why. At least for the time that you're there she'll be okay."

"I am so sorry, Ms. Ramirez, but thank you. By the way, I spoke with Oscar – OJ, last night. He'll be here in a few days."

"Why did you do that? You had no right to say anything to that no good…."

"Ma'am! With all due respect, he is her father and you need help. He could visit her and give Mariela a few more hours of safe time if nothing else."

"Maybe you're right. I just want what's best for my baby."

"I do, too. Thank you again."

I made one more phone call to make sure I would have no trouble at Triple C.

"Irene, its Roger. I'm going up to Triple C. Can you call them and let them know I'm working on the Mariela Ramirez-James matter."

"Roger, what are you doing?"

"I think I'm close to giving you something to work with but I need to speak with her first."

"You're going to have to do better than that."

"I think a bunch of juvenile judges, past and present, are taking kickbacks. They're making money off of Triple C. How's that for a start?"

"Now you're talking. How?"

"Look, it's still fuzzy, but my guess is that Mariela has information that's important but she doesn't know it."

"Okay, I'll call but you better keep me in the loop."

"Okay, you're the boss."

As I was preparing to sign out a car, Thom walked in. He was high fiving people as though he'd just made a basket at the buzzer.

"Roger, did I ever tell you that you're beautiful?"

"I can honestly say no!"

"Well, you are. The *Daubert* motion that we filed was brilliant. Mr. Young is a free man. Once the judge heard all of the testimony he granted our motion immediately. Once the ballistic and finger print evidence was excluded, the government assented to my motion for a directed verdict."

"Congratulations! You pulled another rabbit out of your hat."

"You did buddy! All I had to do was execute. You're a fine lawyer, Roger Work."

"Was, Thom! Was!"

"Hey, dude, I'm not letting you rain on my parade. You did a terrific job and you should be proud."

"Thanks, Thom. I am proud. Right now though, I'm going up to Hillstown Township to visit Mariela at Triple C."

"I forgot. Lenora called telling me to be sure that you used one of our cars. Is she that nervous about the death threat?"

"You know her. What do you think?"

"Good point! Should I come along?"

"No, stay here and celebrate. If I need you, I'll call."

"Alrighty! Please be careful. I don't want Lenora and Richard chewing out my ass."

"I don't plan to do anything stupid."

CHAPTER TWENTY-FOUR

The ride from Center City to Children's Community Center in Hillstown Township was about an hour and a half. When I arrived, I presented my credentials at the security desk. I had to wait twenty minutes before I was able to see Mariela.

When she was brought to me, I could see the fear and uncertainty on her face. The girl was an older version of the picture Bobalu had in his wallet.

"Ms. Ramirez-James, my name is Roger Work. I'm a friend of your father's. He has asked me to find you."

"My daddy sent you. Why? He hasn't had anything to do with us in years."

Roger could see the tears welling up in her eyes.

"May I call you Mariela?"

"Yes!"

"Mariela, I know some things about your father and his past. He's not proud of any of it. When my wife and I were in Key West, we met Mr. James. He learned that we were from Philly and he trusted us with a twenty thousand dollar check made out to you and your mother."

"He did?"

"Yes! Your father is hoping to re-establish a relationship with you and your mom. Whether he succeeds will be up to the three of you. I can only tell you, in my opinion, he regrets what happened in the past and he wants to do right by both of you. In fact, your father will be here in a few days. I called him last night to tell him that you were in a jam."

"My dad is coming to see me?"

"That's right. And if you'll answer some questions maybe you'll be out of here by then."

For the first time Mariela smiled. "What's my dad like? I don't remember much."

"Well, you both have the same facial structure and he's a very good musician. He sings and plays the piano. I don't know what kind of music you like but he's mostly R&B and he's very talented. Do you like music?"

"Yes I do. I've been playing the piano for as long as I can remember."

"I'll bet a week's pay that you're very talented, too."

Mariela blushed. "In some ways it is what I miss most."

"Well, let's see if we can fix that. I've spoken with your mother and your lawyer so it's okay for you to speak with me. If you're at all unsure then before I ask you anything you can check with someone in the front office or a social worker."

"No, that's okay – someone told me you were coming. I was also told that my mother, Ms. Swift and somebody named attorney Roos said that it was okay to talk with you."

"Good! Let's get started. Have you gotten to know any of the other young ladies here?"

"Yes sir, there are a bunch of us from Philly. We talk about things…boyfriends, and how they got here."

"Okay! Are there other young ladies sent here by Judge O'Brien?"

"Yes, how did you know?"

"It was just a guess."

"Do the Philly woman talk about any other judges?"

"Judge Ring, I think that's the name, Judge John Ring."

"Were any other Philly judges mentioned?"

"Yeah, a few, but O'Brien and Ring are the names I hear most."

"Have you heard the name Judge Mara?"

"Yes, sir. He's sent a few here, too."

"How many of them were in your unit?"

"Each unit has about sixty of us. In my unit about half of us were sent here by O'Brien or Ring. I don't know now because I'm living in the medical unit."

"Thank you Mariela. Is there anything else I should know? I'll be leaving within the hour."

"No, Mr. Work. I'm looking forward to seeing my dad."

"That's good because he wants to see you too. He loves you very much."

"Let me ask you a few more questions?" I took my time knowing that these few minutes were precious for Mariela. We talked for another forty five minutes.

* * *

I called Irene from my car.

"Can you check out a few things for me?"

"It depends on what you want."

"How much does a juvenile judge make a year? $125,000 tops? I need to know for sure. Secondly, is there any indication that Judge O'Brien, Mara and Ring are living a lifestyle that seems inconsistent with that kind of income? Their tax returns and home addresses are subject to the Freedom of Information Act. Can you pull that stuff while I drive back?"

"Sure, Roger, I can do that. How is this going to help?"

"If I'm right this is going to be huge. I'll call you as soon as I'm back in the city."

I disconnected.

Twenty minutes later JT called.

"Hey JT what's up?"

"Roger, you asked me to watch your place."

"Yeah."

"Well I went in there around three and there was this fourteen year old Lolita-type in your house."

"What?"

"She said to me, 'Roger, I've missed you. Why did you leave me alone last night? I've been waiting for you. The bed is lonely without you.'"

"JT, are you saying that she thought you were me?"

"You got it. She was doing this whole temptress thing. Then there was banging on the door and some cops forced their way in with a guy who claimed to be the probation officer in charge of the little ho – I mean Sarah. They had me cuffed, just as Miss Bessie barged her way in."

"Bessie said, 'JT, what the heck is going on here? There are TV trucks all over the place and who is this child?' Before I could answer, a policeman, Malloy, I think he's a detective, told her that they were here to arrest Roger Work – pointing to me – for statutory rape of Sarah."

"Miss Bessie went ballistic. 'You all get out of Roger's house. Have you all lost your minds? This man is not Roger Work and this child, or should I say hussy, has never been in this neighborhood or house before today.'"

"Where is everyone now?"

"In your living room. They said I could make one phone call."

"Everything is going to be fine. Is Miss Bessie still there too?"

"Yep."

"Thom will be there in twenty minutes. Just ask the police to wait until he arrives. If they refuse, go peacefully and tell Miss Bessie that everything is under control. These folks may want to do a perp walk with you. But don't worry. If you never trusted me before, do so now."

"Don't you get stupid on me, man, of course I trust you and I'll do as you say."

"Thanks JT – Thom will be there shortly."

I then called Thom.

"Thom, can you and Richard get over to my house on 33rd Street immediately?"

"What's going on?"

"Somebody tried to set me up, but things backfired. These folks are desperate. The police are holding JT and a minor named Sarah. When the police entered they thought JT was me. I'm sure there's a recording of everything said, too. I want Richard with you, just in case you need a warrant or some kind of court order as soon as you arrive."

"Okay, we'll be there in twenty. Does this have anything to do with what we were talking about on Friday?"

"I'll bet you a double cheesesteak it does!"

"Hey man, there's no need to be cruel. I said I'm on it."

"One double cheesesteak coming up."

"With extra onions?"

CHAPTER TWENTY-FIVE

Pushing past television crews, I arrived at my 33rd Street home about forty minutes after speaking with Thom. I was armed with a large cheese-steak sandwich with extra onions. Thom accepted my offering with the glee of a child on Christmas morning. Richard had a look of horror on his face as Thom bit into his treat.

The officer in charge asked, “Who are you?”

“Roger Work! This is my house and I’d like you and that young lady to leave.”

“Mr. Work, we have a warrant for your arrest.”

“May I see it officer?”

Detective Malloy handed him the document. “I see this was issued by Judge Ring. Richard would you take a look at this?”

“Wait a minute who is this guy?”

Richard produced his credentials. Malloy said “I’m sorry. I had no idea your honor. Can you please tell me what’s going on?”

“Richard, can I try to sort this out?” I asked.

“Please do!”

“Young lady what’s your name?”

“Sarah.”

“Sarah, before coming to my house, where did you live?”

“Do you mean my address or where I’d been staying?”

“Where you’d been staying?”

“I was in Bucks County at Triple C.”

“How long had you been there?”

“Judge O’Brien sent me there four months ago.”

I asked, “How long was your sentence?”

“Nine months. But the judge promised I’d be released in a few days if I came here and spent some time with you.”

“One more question. How did you get here?”

“Judge O’Brien sent some guy to pick me up and bring me here.”

"Oh Lord" cried Miss Bessie.

"Thank you, Sarah. Richard and Thom, do you have any ideas? Officer Malloy is looking for some direction."

Richard turned to Malloy, "Please take this young woman to Unity House for the moment and make sure that someone stays with her. You'll have a written order from me by fax in fifteen minutes."

"Yes your honor. But, what about this warrant?"

"I'm going to do you a favor and void it right now."

"Your honor, I've never had this happen before."

"Thank God! I've never done this either, but this is far better than the city or you being sued for violating Mr. Work's civil rights by that guy over there stuffing that disgusting steak sandwich in his mouth."

"Judge, I am still not sure I understand what's going on here."

"I don't know either but it's clear that Mr. Work should not be arrested. So do as I've asked."

"Yes, your honor."

Just then, the probation officer, Paul Todd's phone buzzed, "Hello. Yes, Judge O'Brien, they are both here. I can't do that, your honor. Judge Richard Allen is here and he's ordered us to stand down. Do you want to talk to him?"

The lack of additional sound from the phone made it clear the Mr. Todd's conversation with Judge O'Brien had ended.

Sarah, Todd and Detective Malloy left the house with the press in hot pursuit.

After the police left my home, I reassured Miss Bessie everything was fine.

"Roger that was terrible what the policeman was saying about you. What are you going to do about it?"

"Miss Bessie, I'm going to go downtown with my lawyer, Thom, and make sure that this doesn't happen again. Are you okay?"

"Child, I'm fine. This mess just upsets me."

"JT is going to walk you home. I'll call you in the morning. Okay?"

"Thank you."

Bessie and JT departed. I then turned to Thom and Richard. Before heading into town, Richard suggested I call Irene and Lenora. He pointed out that Lenora might see something on the news so letting her know what had transpired was a good idea. “Thanks Richard.”

I got Lenora’s voicemail. “Honey, there was an incident at the house. Everything is fine. But you may see something on TV. I should be home in a couple of hours. I’m with Thom and Richard. Love you. Bye.”

CHAPTER TWENTY-SIX

I called Irene. "Irene, did you locate any of the tax or real estate information on Judge O'Brien? You did! Let me put you on speaker. Thom and Richard are with me."

"Hi Thom, Hi Richard. Roger, according to his tax returns the O'Brien's annual gross is 160K. Their home is nothing special. But Mrs. O'Brien owns vacation property in Aspen, Colorado and Captiva, Florida. The estimated value is in excess of a million."

"Really?"

"Roger, guys, Mrs. O'Brien has never made more than forty thousand a year and she's not from a wealthy family. Do any of you believe in coincidences?"

"No!" We all said in unison.

"Neither do I. According to what I've found, these real estate transactions started about the time Triple C came on line. Surprise, right? The homes were paid for in cash."

"Irene, cut to the chase!"

"I'd bet a bucketful of Benjamin's that O'Brien is getting kickbacks from Triple C. Every time he sends a kid there he gets a gratuity. How much, I can't say. Perhaps $10,000 per child. This would explain how his wife can afford property in two of the most exclusive vacation spots in the country."

"Can you fax what you have to our office?" asked Thom.

"Sure."

"Irene?

"Yes, Roger.

"I hope your office will consider some kind of class action on behalf of the children detained at Triple C. Those greedy pigs should not be allowed to get away with what they did."

"I've already started."

"Good! I'm going to talk with Mariela's mother and her attorney. With any luck, Ms. Swift can get her a hearing immediately. We've got enough to show probable cause that O'Brien was sending children to Triple C for profit. I think that's a violation of due process. What do you guys think?"

Thom laughed, "Can you say 1983?" 42 United States Code Section 1983 is often used to address situations where government officials have intentionally violated the Civil Rights of an individual or group.

Irene responded, "That's what I was thinking. This guy violated the civil rights of God-only-knows how many children, just to show that he was a big shot. This is sickening. What a hypocrite. I've heard a few of his law-and-order chats with children. This bastard should be placed under the jail."

I chimed in, "I agree. We should all do what we can to make that happen."

"I can't believe my colleagues would misuse their power this way. I'll call the U.S. Attorney and the State Attorney General's offices."

"Irene, Thanks you've done a great job."

"You saw this before everyone, Roger, you deserve the credit."

"I don't care about credit. Just get those young ladies out of their modern day Charles Dicken's nightmare and back home where they belong."

* * *

CHAPTER TWENTY-SEVEN

Once Richard spoke with the U.S. Attorney, State Attorney General, Philly's District Attorney and the President Judge, all charges related to me disappeared. The District Attorney promised to convene a Grand Jury in a week to look into the activities of Judges Ring, O'Brien and Mara, and the owners of Children's Community Center. I told them about Mariela as well.

"Please, do what you can to get that little girl out of that hellhole."

Both the DA and President Judge promised to do so immediately.

As I was leaving the meeting, I inadvertently ran into the police officer who had attempted to arrest me earlier. Officer Malloy apologized and begged that I not sue. "Forget about it. You made a mistake. That is not a crime. Can you point me in the direction of Detective Abbott's office?"

Clearly relieved, he pointed to the left and said, "Thanks."

* * *

Thomasina Abbott, Chief of Detectives, had taken over the initial investigation of Judges Ring, O'Brien, Mara and others tied to Children's Community Center.

Detective Abbott's name was associated with a rash of serial killings in Philly more than two years ago. Abbott had headed the special taskforce charged with finding the serial killer. The highest ranking black woman on the force now, Detective Abbott was a proud graduate of the Philadelphia Public School System. She was quick to acknowledge that her love of track and field played a significant role in her staying out of trouble as a teenager. Detective Abbott got lucky with the serial murders when a mystery voice bailed Abbott and the entire department out of a real jam. The actual killer's body was found floating in the Delaware River. He supposedly died of natural causes. When working in law enforcement, one must have a sense of humor. His co-defendant, Tony Donatelli pled after being delivered to Abbott on a silver platter. Abbott would never forget the voice on the phone. The caller told her it was over. And that's exactly what happened. The killings stopped just as suddenly as they had started. She would be eternally grateful to that voice. Abbott became a folk hero of sorts.

While interviewing me, Abbott received a call from that mysterious voice.

"Detective Abbott, do you remember me?"

"Yes!"

"Listen carefully, Mr. Work did nothing wrong. Those bastards wanted me to kill him. Judge O'Brien, Ring, Mara and those other sorry excuses for public officials are pigs. They are so dirty I can smell the stench from here. They've been taking kickbacks for years. Triple C was a sham. An excuse to lock up kids and make a few bucks."

"How do you know these things?"

The speaker laughed, "Goodbye, Detective, and good luck. The next time we talk maybe you'll be police commissioner."

Then there was a click and the phone line went quiet. Next, you heard the dial tone. A shell-shocked Abbott turned to me, "Mr. Work, you can go. Thanks for your help."

* * *

CHAPTER TWENTY-EIGHT

While I was wrapping things up on my end, Irene and her staff worked quickly to draft the necessary documents to file in Federal District Court located at 4th and Market Streets in Center City. The court house was just a stone's throw from Independence Hall. This was the place where the Declaration of Independence was hammered out by a group of people who understood the value of liberty and freedom. The irony was not lost on anyone. Irene believed this was a sign. They had a righteous law suit for a righteous cause.

In the legal documents Irene argued, Children's Community Center, its officers and Judges Mara, O'Brien and Ring along with others unknown conspired to violate the Civil Rights of, yet to be named, numerous children.

Mariela was named the lead plaintiff. In *Mariela and Other Unknown Juveniles v. Children's Community Center et al*, Irene sought damages and immediate injunctive relief. Litigation involving juveniles rarely are captioned with the child's real or full name. She demanded all the children be freed immediately and that Children's Community Center be closed. The Commonwealth of Pennsylvania represented by an Assistant State Attorney General did not oppose the request.

Irene was surprised. She had been itching for a fight. But like every good lawyer, she knew not to turn her back on a gift. Judge David Nelson, with the consent of the parties, allowed the motion and granted an order releasing all the children. His order also stated CCC was to be closed before midnight. As Irene rushed from the court room with the order in hand, she asked her staff to start contacting parents. She personally called Juanita to tell her the good news. Bobalu was with her. Irene told them to meet her in Hillstown at the Upper Bucks County facility.

State Police Officers escorted Irene to Triple C. With troopers standing at her side, she served Judge Nelson's order on Warden Katherine Payne. At first, Warden Payne protested. However, the presence of steely-eyed troopers caused any idea of resisting to evaporate into the evening air.

Parents who lived in nearby communities were waiting for Irene. As she watched parents and children being reunited, her eyes welled with tears of joy and pride. Around nine, she called Roger.

"It's crazy up here. Children are everywhere. I've never seen so many happy people. It's like Christmas morning. The children and parents are all hugging me and saying thank you. They should be thanking you."

"What you're doing is thanks enough."

"How could we all let things get so bad?"

"I don't know but tonight everything is right. Take a bow and we'll talk once the dust settles. Enjoy the evening. By the way, I'm proud to know you Counselor."

She responded, "Back at you!"

Roger hung up. Lenora asked, "Was that Irene?"

"Yeah babe! The hellhole has been closed and most of the children are with their families. A few will temporarily end up in foster care. Not everyone has family to go to right now. We'll have to keep and eye on things to make sure the children are not going from the frying pan and into the fire."

Lenora gave Roger a kiss. "Good job, big guy."

CHAPTER TWENTY-NINE

Mariela was reunited with both of her parents the evening Irene arrived at Hillstown. All the other children held at Triple C were either released or transferred to other facilities. Irene's office was in the process of filing a class action on behalf of all of the children who had ever been sent to Triple C. By the next afternoon, the defendants, all the current and former judges involved in the operation from Philadelphia, Bucks and Delaware Counties, faces and names were plastered all over television and newspapers. The story had legs. It went viral. The national press was interested in the terrible abuse of power that had occurred in the Cradle of Liberty.

A week after the events on 33rd Street, indictments were announced charging Judges O'Brien, Ring, Mara and others with conspiracy and illegally accepting kickbacks. There were numerous rumors that Judge Mara had agreed to testify against his co-conspirators in exchange for a light sentence. The rats were abandoning a sinking ship. As the adage goes, "there's no honor among thieves."

But it was Judge O'Brien who won the race to the top. He was the first to cut a deal with prosecutors. No conditions were, in fact, agreed upon except the District Attorney promised to give consideration to the defrocked judge at the time of his sentencing after he had testified against the others.

CHAPTER THIRTY

On the following Saturday, JT, Third, Thom, Richard, Brandi, Lenora and I hosted the surprise eighty-fifth birthday party for Miss Bessie. When Bessie walked into the house, we all began singing Stevie Wonder's song, "*Happy Birthday to you, Happy Birthday.*" The song was composed in recognition of Dr. Martin Luther King Jr's birthday becoming a holiday. Everyone had a gift for her. We waited until everyone had given her their gifts to present ours.

Bessie said, "Roger, what is this?"

"Open it!"

Miss Bessie was initially shocked and then started laughing as she saw what Lenora and I had given her. Bessie held up the record jacket, "Bessie Smith Live at Tally Ho," circa 1960.

"Happy Birthday, Miss Bessie".

Holding up the record, Miss Bessie asked, "Lord, child, where did you find this old thing?"

"After Key West, I was determined to find a copy. I got lucky. It's amazing what you can find online today."

"We were both in our mid-thirties in 1960. I had forgotten all about this."

"How did you and Grandma end up in the music business?"

"Sadie and I always sang in church. She had a beautiful voice. But she was shy. We'd take turns singing lead on some of those old gospel songs. One Sunday morning this good looking guy came up to us after the service. 'Have you lady's ever thought about doing a night club act?' We laughed and said no."

"So what happened?"

"Sadie and I got to talking and convinced ourselves that it might be fun." Bessie smiled, "We wanted to be on the Ed Sullivan Show. Do you remember that?"

"Yes! Every Sunday night I recall, on CBS."

"That's right."

"Did you ever make it?"

"No, but we still had fun."

Bessie continued, "Until I saw this here picture, I had forgotten that we were two attractive women, don't you think?"

"Absolutely."

"Do you remember the Tally Ho Club, Roger?"

"No. I'm not sure that I even knew there was one until I saw this."

"Well, Tally Ho was this fancy supper night club up in Valley Forge. Lots of big-name entertainers appeared there. We were so excited, child, it took us almost a month to find just the right outfits."

"You both looked stunning."

"Thanks! Lenora, you've trained him right."

"Now, Miss Bessie, you know I was domesticated before meeting Lenora."

"I suppose. Still, I can see a big improvement."

"So what happened? How did you end up making this record?"

"We were scheduled to be the warm-up act for Count Basie. He was a real charmer. Basie was doing a live recording of his show. His people used us to make sure that the recording equipment was working properly. We usually did four or five songs in our set. I guess they recorded the last two."

"Well Miss Bessie, I don't know about you but we're all dying to hear it."

"Well."

Given the years that had passed, the recording was clear. For a moment we were all transported back to the Tally Ho in 1960. Miss Bessie started, "God Bless the Child." At one point, I could hear Grandma harmonizing with her! Tears ran down my eyes. Lenora, Thom, Richard, Third, Brandi and JT were in awe.

Miss Bessie started tapping her toe. The second song, *"Someone to Watch Over Me,"* was even better.

Once the music died, everyone was silent. Lenora finally broke the ice. "Miss Bessie, that was wonderful. Thank you for sharing a bit of your past with us. It was a real treat."

"See, Roger. That woman has class and good taste. Thank you, sweetie. This may be my best birthday ever."

EPILOGUE

As the weeks passed, things returned to normal at the Defender's Association. Thom and I were happy to get back to our usual fare of robberies, burglaries and other crimes.

During spring break, Malik returned to the office for a few days. I filled him in on the Triple C matter. Malik had followed the news coverage online.

"Roger, I never saw our office or your name being referenced in any of those stories. What a mess."

"Malik, soon you'll learn that it's not always a good idea to have your name associated with a story in the news."

As the men were talking Lenora knocked on my door, "Is this a boy's only club?"

"Honey, what are you doing here?"

"That's for me to know and you to find out, fella."

Within minutes there was an announcement from Angela over the intercom system asking everyone to report to the conference room.

"Sorry, honey but we've got to go."

"That's okay!"

By the time Malik and I arrived almost everybody seemed to be in place, with the exception of Thom.

Sarcastically, I asked, "Where's our fearless leader?" As the last word of my sentence came rolling out of my mouth, Thom stepped into the room. Lenora was at his side.

"Good morning, everyone!" I received a letter from Governor Rendell yesterday. He has asked me to share his message with everyone. Let me begin."

Richard also slipped into the conference room.

"I, Governor Edward Rendell, in recognition of numerous contributions to the people of this Commonwealth made by former Attorney Roger Work of North Philadelphia, now a paralegal and investigator with the Philadelphia Defender's Association, I hereby declare that the petition for a pardon filed on behalf of Mr. Work by Attorneys Thom Dean, Irene Roos and the Honorable Richard Allen, has been granted effective this date, Tuesday, April 4, 2009. Mr. Work is no longer deemed to be a risk to society. Any crimes committed in Pennsylvania are pardoned. I sincerely hope that Mr. Work will apply for reinstatement of his license to practice law. He is now a citizen in good standing and a person of outstanding character. The people of this Commonwealth need zealous, competent and compassionate advocates like Mr. Work.

Signed: Governor Edward Rendell."

Everyone clapped while Lenora hugged me. "I am so proud and happy for you."

"Did you know about this?"

"Of course. You deserve this, Roger. You're one of the most honorable men I've ever known. Congratulations."

Malik also hugged me. "After I graduate from law school we can open a practice together."

"I look forward to that, Malik."

Thom walked over to me. "You've earned this Roger. I felt obligated to try. If I had asked, your answer would have been no. Lenora, Richard, Irene, in fact, all of us believed you deserve a second chance. Good luck."

"Thom, I don't know what to say." Lenora reached up kissed my cheek and whispered, "Just say, thank you, Thom."

"Thank you, Thom."

Some present in the conference room laughed while others cried.

I just smiled and tried to soak up the affection I felt from my wife and friends.

* * *

When Lenora and I returned home after the day-long celebration, we picked up our mail. Sorting through it there was an envelope postmarked Key West, Florida. Inside was a plain sheet of paper.

Roger and Lenora,

Thank You.

Sincerely,

OJ

Inside the envelope was a photograph of OJ, Juanita and Mariela standing in Mallory Square at sunset.

* * *

Almost after a year to the day, Children's Community Center was closed, a jury convicted Ring, Mara and the others of a laundry list of crimes. Each defendant was sentenced to a term of thirty years to life. Mr. O'Brien, the government's star witness, in exchange for his cooperation, received a prison sentence of twenty years with the possibility of parole after serving twelve of his twenty year sentence.

The "Children of CCC," as the media referred to them, had a part of their childhood stolen by people who were in a position of trust. No verdict or sentence would ever give them back what was taken under color of law. They would have to be satisfied knowing it was the law that injured them, but also the law that freed them and restored their good names. Mariela was perhaps the best example.

At a joint press conference, the District Attorney, flanked by the State Attorney General and the United States Attorney General, applauded the verdicts. They pledged in a written statement: "We will review all privatization contracts used by the state to make sure that something like this never occurs again."

Acknowledgements

This story is a work of fiction. To the extent it may mirror events that actually occurred is a coincidence.

I am fortunate to have colleagues and friends who are generous with their ideas, time and support. This story proves that everybody needs a community of friends if we are to continue to grow as lifelong learners.

Thank you to Donna Desirey, my former Administrative Assistant and dear friend. Ms. Desirey has worked with me from the very start of the adventures of Roger Work. Lots of other good friends have offered ideas and critiques to various drafts of this story. You all know who you are. Thank you!

If you have never spent time in Philadelphia then you ought to do so. You are missing some of the finest artwork in the world. Thank you to Amy Johnston and the artists of the Philadelphia Mural Arts Program. I am privileged to be able to share your powerful story. The murals you see in this book, along with 2,500 others, can be seen throughout the city. Each is unique and inspirational. Perhaps, more importantly, every mural is the product of the artist and the members of the neighborhood where these works appear. Each mural is proof that hope still lives in urban America.

When the people of a community come together that, in itself, is a beautiful thing.

The Mural appearing on the cover was created by Donald Gensler. It is entitled: "Embrace: Second Chance." Thank you, Mr. Gensler, for allowing me to use your work with the cooperation of the City of Philadelphia Mural Arts Program.

Last, but not least, I wish to thank my wife, Ele. She is a loving and demanding taskmaster. Because of both, this book is far better than anything I might have written alone.

Since I have not lived in Philly for years, some of my descriptions of places and locations may not be accurate. I am always interested in learning. The reader can reach me at Sheriff3@comcast.net.

ABOUT THE AUTHOR

Robert V. Ward, Jr. was born in Philadelphia, Pennsylvania. He has lived in Boston since 1968. He is married and resides on Boston's South Shore with his wife of thirty-two years. Professor Ward has taught Criminal Law, Criminal Procedure, Prisoner's Rights, Evidence and Race and Law. He is the former dean of the University of Massachusetts School Law –Dartmouth, formerly the Southern New England School of Law.

This is Robert Ward's third book in the novella series about disbarred lawyer, Roger Work.

www.ingramcontent.com/pod-product-compliance
Ingram Content Group UK Ltd.
Pitfield, Milton Keynes, MK11 3LW, UK
UKHW041936190726
13854UKWH00004B/1616